GUNSMOKE IN A COLORADO CANYON

Squatting on a ridge in the Colorado Mountains, his quarry hidden in the black of the night, the temperature down to freezing and falling rapidly, Will Foreman cursed his own impetuosity. Lured by the glint of a rifle barrel in the last rays of the dying sun, Foreman was trapped. Does he sit it out and risk being frozen to death, or chance a bullet in the back as he climbs down the mountainside in the dark? Foreman is on the wrong end of a deadly cat and mouse game.

Books by Bret Rey
in the Linford Western Library:

TROUBLE VALLEY
RUNAWAY
MARSHAL WITHOUT A BADGE

BRET REY

GUNSMOKE IN A COLORADO CANYON

Complete and Unabridged

LINFORD
Leicester

First published in Great Britain in 1991 by
Robert Hale Limited
London

First Linford Edition
published October 1993
by arrangement with
Robert Hale Limited
London

British Library CIP Data

Rey, Bret
   Gunsmoke in a Colorado canyon.
   —Large print ed.—
   Linford western library
   I. Title II. Series
   823.914 [F]

   ISBN 0–7089–7440–6

Published by
F. A. Thorpe (Publishing) Ltd.
Anstey, Leicestershire

Set by Words & Graphics Ltd.
Anstey, Leicestershire
Printed and bound in Great Britain by
T. J. Press (Padstow) Ltd., Padstow, Cornwall

This book is printed on acid-free paper

For
Bruce
who enjoys the chase

1

WILL FOREMAN pressed the rifle-stock hard into his shoulder, facial muscles tightening, forefinger clawing the trigger, lying perfectly still as shadows wavered on the night wind. Then the quarry disappeared once more, just as Will had been ready to fire. The night stalker was bent on sending shivers of fear gnawing at his insides and, Will allowed, he had succeeded. He wished he knew which one of the two outlaws it was, Eddie Arnold or Randolph Carter, even though he acknowledged that it made little difference. Both men were intent on killing him and his ageing partner, Keith Jackson.

Will cursed himself inwardly, knowing that once again he had ignored Jackson's advice, adding to another missed chance.

"Only a fool goes charging into battle without a plan," Jackson had counselled him more than once.

Eyes raking the shadows, he had time to reflect on his impulsive decision to leave Jackson down below and climb up the canyon side in search of the man whose rifle had glinted just once in the last rays of the sun. Now night had enveloped him and, somehow, the outlaw had spotted him and gained the advantage. Will could not rid himself of the suspicion that he had been lured into a trap. It was precisely what the old man had feared.

"Just watch yourself, Will! Whichever one it is may have spotted us. If he has, he'll watch your every step."

"Cover me."

The long climb had been tortuous, a strain on his leg muscles, and entailed frequent pauses to pull air into his lungs. In concentrating on a safe climb by a zig-zag route, he had lost his sense of direction, surrendering any hope he had of coming up behind the sniper.

Now the tables were turned and the chill of fear had traversed Will's spine with every unusual sound. Crouched as he was in the cleft of two jutting rocks, he had the unnerving feeling that the night stalker was playing cat-and-mouse with him, revelling in the prospect of filling him with lead.

He wondered what Jackson had done after the darkness shrouded the canyon. Had he been able to follow Will's progress while the light lasted, or lost him in the twists and turns Will had been obliged to make to ensure safe footing?

Where was Keith Jackson now?

Gun thunder bounced off the walls of the canyon with a suddenness that startled Will Foreman.

It had come from down below and could mean only one thing . . . Keith Jackson and the other outlaw had encountered each other, but at what distance? More than seven years as Jackson's side-kick had induced the feeling that the old man was immortal, indestructible. When the gunsmoke cleared Will was confident there would be only one of the two fugitives to contend with. He settled himself again, ears pricked and eyes peering into the shadows.

The chill of night began to creep into his flesh, reminding him how cold the Colorado Mountains could become once the sun had cast its rays on the other side of the world. Like the damn fool he was, he had left his warm coat tied behind his saddle in the stupid belief that his mission to seek out the outlaw would not take long. "The impetuosity of youth," Jackson had remarked on several occasions, "is the enemy of wisdom." How right the old man was.

Will shivered in the lowering temperature, desperately wanting to get down to level ground again but afraid to move and give away his new position. The outlaw had fired at him five times, and three of the shots had come much too close for comfort.

Unless he is a rank bad shot, a sniper can only miss his target with a rifle so many times; eventually a man of Will Foreman's size is going to be too big to miss.

Where the hell are you?

Will's anxiety was eating into his confidence. Did Eddie Arnold — or was it Randolph Carter? — know his position, and yet feared giving away his own in an attempt to end the life of the young Pinkerton agent?

Damn him! If he doesn't move soon we'll both freeze to death up here, Will decided. The prospect would prompt him to take the initiative again if nothing happened soon. Even a bullet in the back was preferable to a slow death in the icy blast that had begun to blow through the jagged rocks.

There was something odd, something Will could not fathom, about the whole situation. Why had the two outlaws separated, one remaining down below while the other climbed the sloping side of the canyon? Eddie Arnold and

Randolph Carter had been the only two of the gang to escape from the railroad robbery, the other gang members all killed or badly wounded by Pinkerton agents in a shoot-out, so why had the two survivors separated now after sticking together for all those weeks since the hold-up?

Was it part of a strategy to isolate Will from Jackson, thinking that by separating the two Pinkerton men they could pick them off one at a time? Maybe it had been no more than a ploy to get a better look at the men following their trail, but whatever, it had succeeded in getting Will alone up on the mountain.

Instructed to hunt down the escaped robbers, Jackson and Will Foreman had followed trail for weeks, frustrated three times when they thought they were getting close. Finally spotting them heading into this deep canyon, they had followed with a fresh surge of hope, confident that Arnold and Carter had at last made the one big mistake that was usually all that was needed for men outside the law to find themselves trapped.

Now it was Will Foreman who was trapped.

As he crouched with growing impatience, thoughts of those frustrating days did nothing to cheer him.

His anger escalated as he began to shake with the now freezing temperature. It was no use, he could remain there no longer. If he didn't make a move and get his muscles working again his blood would turn to ice water in his veins. The danger of climbing down a mountainside in the inky blackness was preferable to the fear of being shot in the back or turned into a frozen statue.

It was a slow and arduous return. Every time a foot slipped his heart pounded mercilessly, but no shot disturbed the stillness and, after almost two hours, he was down on the canyon floor again. Either the night stalker had made the same decision as Will — but done it much earlier — or had weighed the risk of his own gun-flame being sighted and put the safety catch back on his rifle in his anxiety to find out if his pard had survived the gunfight below him.

Will Foreman felt no qualms on that score. Keith Jackson would be waiting with his victim somewhere near his own horse, but just how far away that was became impossible to estimate, with Will not knowing precisely where he had reached safe ground again. His bearings completely lost during his descent, he now had to concede he could be as much as a mile, or even two, away from where he had picketed his roan.

He began to walk stealthily southwards, wary in case the man who had waited up on the mountain for him was aware of his present position. Except for the howling of the wind the canyon was eerily quiet. No coyotes called, no owls hooted, and what creatures of the night were out on their regular hunt for food were doing it with their customary quiet stealth.

He was suddenly startled by a cry of terror rending the night air. It was such a piercing cry that he shivered in revulsion at the thought of the victim held in the jaws of a larger carnivore, soon to be torn apart in the easing of animal hunger.

He continued on his way back to his horse and the waiting Keith Jackson on leaden legs, aching in every fibre. The climb up the mountain and down again had wearied him to the brink of exhaustion. His boots and clothing were scuffed and dirty but he no longer cared.

A horse whinnied.

He froze in his tracks, knowing the animal was not his own. Neither did he think it was Jackson's buckskin. It must belong to either Eddie Arnold or Randolph Carter. Had the whinny been a greeting or a warning? If it was a warning, then the thread of life was beginning to look thin again.

Forewarned, whichever of those two outlaws had survived until now might well have his rifle pointing in Will Foreman's direction, waiting for him to come closer, and the opportunity to make shot number six a killer.

2

PATIENCE had never been a virtue in Will Foreman's make-up and seven and a half years with Keith Jackson had only partially remedied the failing. He knew full well that Jackson had been right in teaching him that a long wait so often provides worthwhile dividends. The difference between living and dying was often decided by which adversary became frustrated with waiting for the other to make his move.

Now, in the freezing night, the one thing that could give away a man's position was the grey-white puff of expended breath from his nostrils. Standing perfectly still, controlling his breathing, Will weighed the possibility, and decided it was a risk worth taking. Crouching low, he moved forward on cat-soft feet, eyes straining for the sight of man or horse.

The horse whinnied softly once more and he knew it was no more than a dozen yards away.

Why no sudden burst of gunfire? Surely the man must have spotted him if he was anywhere near his horse!

The silence was total. Gradually, as he peered into the gloom, his eyes picked out the equine shape a little to his left, but there was no sign of a man.

He moved stealthily towards the horse as it pawed the ground and bobbed its head in greeting. It was the dappled grey that Randolph Carter had been riding, but where was Carter? The answer came to him in a flash of realization, it was Carter who had tangled with Keith Jackson while Will had been seeking and was being sought by Eddie Arnold. It was Arnold who had stalked him up on the mountain. Carter was dead.

The dappled grey would be needed to carry its owner to the nearest town with a law office. As the tension drained out of Will Foreman's muscles he debated the wisdom of taking the horse with him. If Eddie Arnold was anywhere near, the danger of discovery would increase if Will took the grey along. The sound of shod hooves carries a long way in the still of night.

He tried to estimate how far away Keith Jackson was, but the darkness was almost total and it was impossible to pin-point his position.

His mind made up, he unpicketed the horse and led it south, having decided it could become a shield between him and his stalker if the need should arise.

He stopped to listen as an owl-hoot came to his ears. The hoot was repeated twice and Will knew that Keith Jackson was not far away. The sound would have fooled most men, but Will was well accustomed to the signal he and the old man had perfected over the years.

Another hundred yards further on and the call was wafted on the night air again, and this time Will Foreman answered with a single hoot, slightly higher pitched. It took him several minutes to locate Jackson, but the relief was so enormous that Will permitted himself a wide grin of pleasure.

"You got Carter then," he said without a note of doubt in his voice.

"I got him. That his horse you've gotten there?"

Will nodded. "Dappled grey."

"We'll need that come morning. Best go and get your bedroll or you'll freeze to death."

Will shivered and thought of his warm coat. "I'll do that."

"You were a damn fool to climb up there without your coat."

"I know."

"You get Arnold?"

"No, but he damn near got me three times. After the noise you made down here, I figured he came down to investigate. Looks like you've not seen him."

Jackson figured Will's last comment

14

did not call for any response and he closed his eyes. "Get some shut-eye, Will."

Will noticed that Jackson had settled himself into his soogans, head resting against a boulder. The old man always slept in a half-sitting position when they had to camp out at night.

Quietly, Will made his way to the roan he had left several hours earlier. Frost had already settled on his rolled coat. He shook it out and put it on, then carried his bedroll to unfurl alongside his mentor.

* * *

The moon hung in the dawn sky when he awoke, surprised that he had ever managed to fall asleep on the frozen ground, an indication of the extent of his exhaustion. He uncoiled his long body and went in search of wood to light a fire. By the time he had gathered sufficient the new day had arrived, diminishing the danger of the flames being spotted by Eddie Arnold. The boulders surrounding the spot Keith Jackson had selected to spend the night would also offer a shield against searching eyes.

Where was Arnold now?

Jackson's eyes were still closed when Will took him his mug of coffee. "Mr Jackson."

Will waved the strong-smelling java under the old man's nose and slowly his eyes opened. The spark Will normally associated with Jackson was missing. Something was sadly wrong.

"You all right, Mr Jackson? You look kinda sick."

The rate of Will's heartbeat quickened as he waited for an answer. When it came it sent shivers of alarm coursing through his veins.

"I've been gut-shot, Will."

Will's hand shook, spilling some of the coffee, as Jackson's simple statement induced a kind of disturbance in Will's mind he had experienced only rarely before. Keith Jackson gut-shot?

It hardly seemed possible. He was too wily a bird to have allowed Randolph Carter to get the drop on him. No man ever lived who could out-smart Keith Jackson. That was why he had survived so long. The old man was joshing him.

But even as the thought came to him it began to die. Jackson would never joke about anything so serious and the dull eyes confirmed it.

"You hurt bad, Mr Jackson?"

"I've lived through the night, so I reckon it can't be too bad." He lifted his right hand. "I'll take that coffee now, but don't fix me any breakfast. I feel too sick to eat."

"Best let me take a look at the wound."

"Later, son. You get yourself something to eat. You'll need it, but keep your eyes peeled for Eddie Arnold. He's still around some place, unless he fell off that crag up there."

A thought came to Will. He looked around in vain. "Where's Carter? I thought you said you'd gotten him?"

"I did. He's a couple of hundred yards up the canyon. I crawled back here in case Arnold knew where to find him. Don't worry about Carter; he'll keep until you've gotten his pard."

"You sure I cain't do nothin' for you right now?"

"Feed yourself, then settle down to wait for Arnold to show himself."

Will summoned a grin. "He could've frozen to death up yonder."

"No, he's too wily for that. He'll find Carter, then come looking for us."

So the old man had left Carter where he could easily be spotted. Now he was counting on Will to end the chase after the two outlaws by getting Eddie Arnold, only Will did not quite share Jackson's confidence in Arnold's response to the killing of his friend. Once Arnold found his dead buddy he would be more likely to disappear in a hurry, rather than go hunting the two Pinkerton men.

Mist lay deep on the peaks of the

mountain. Will wondered how long it would be before the sun broke through, but already the hot coffee and the food in his belly had thawed the chill in his blood. He itched to get back to hunting Eddie Arnold.

"Mr Jackson."

The old eyes slowly opened again and Will knew that Jackson was wounded more seriously than he had admitted.

"Want me to take a look at that wound?"

"Later. When the sun comes through. I'm fairly comfortable right now."

"Uhuh." Will guessed Jackson was afraid of being moved. "I'll go an' look for the body."

"It's out in the open, near a big boulder. Watch out for Arnold."

"I will. Sure you'll be all right 'til I get back?"

"If you don't get yourself killed."

Will grinned reassurance. "I ain't spent more'n seven years alongside you without learnin' somethin'."

He reached for his rifle and headed

further into the canyon. As Jackson had taught him, he tried putting himself into the mind of the fugitive, attempting to assess what Eddie Arnold had done last night and what he might do now. He knew the old man was right when he opined Arnold had more sense than freeze to death up on that crag, and if he had fallen as he climbed down in the darkness, surely his anguished cry would have reached one of them. He might, however, have injured himself half-way down. In that event, he would not yet have found his partner's body, which Will estimated would be frozen solid by now.

His cautious approach accounted for the lapse of fifteen minutes before he saw the corpse lying almost full-stretch on the hard ground.

★ ★ ★

The sun broke through the mist during his long vigil. Secreted under an overhang of rock, with boulders in front of him to shield his presence while still having a clear view of the body, his patience began to wear thin. Where was Eddie Arnold? Had he found the body himself last night or early this morning and already made his getaway? The possibility rankled in Will's mind, until he recalled there was only one way into this deep canyon.

During their initial examination of the rugged terrain the day before, he and Jackson had satisfied themselves that the floor of the canyon rose gradually until it petered out in high rock strata, roughly two and a half miles north. To get out any other way, Eddie Arnold would have needed to be a mountain lion, and there was no way he could ride a horse away other than by the same route by which he had entered the canyon with Carter.

Why had Arnold's horse not been picketed alongside Carter's? The two men must have decided to separate in their determination to pick off their pursuers with rifle-shots. They had damn near succeeded, too, Will mused angrily. Carter must have gotten sight of Jackson before the old man had managed to loose off the shots that ended the outlaw's run of good fortune.

He began to worry about Jackson. Shouldn't he be trying to get the old man to a doctor instead of worrying about Eddie Arnold? If Jackson died on the journey back to civilization, Will would never forgive himself. That possibility helped him to decide on his next step, but even as he stood up to move away he saw Eddie Arnold leading his horse towards the corpse.

3

HE stood perfectly still, every nerve tingling in the aftermath of Eddie Arnold's sudden appearance. For more than an hour he had waited patiently for something to happen, then, just as he was on the point of returning to Keith Jackson, Arnold had come into view. It was not long before Arnold spotted the dead body of his partner. His eyes searched the vicinity as he halted in fear, his right hand fisting the revolver from its holster.

Will Foreman watched as he tried to decide how to tackle the outlaw. Killing him would be easy; he was a sitting-duck target, but that would have been cold-blooded murder and contrary to Pinkerton rules of operation. Outlaws should be taken prisoner whenever possible and killed only when an operative's own life was threatened.

Arnold moved towards the body with extreme caution, eyes flicking first one way and then another, alert in case he was walking into a trap, but then, satisfied there was no immediate danger, he bent over the corpse. He touched Randolph Carter's cheek, then withdrew his hand far more quickly than he had stretched it out. Surely he must have suspected his partner might have been killed the night before, Will mused, recalling the sound of blazing guns when he and Arnold were up on the mountain top.

Will watched Arnold considering his options. Would he leave the body for the buzzards and the coyotes or would he look for Carter's horse to take it away? The odds against him making any attempt to bury Carter must have been mighty high. It was extremely doubtful that Arnold carried a shovel and, in any case, the ground was bone-hard and digging a grave would have been an arduous task.

Arnold climbed suddenly into his saddle and turned the horse to face the mouth of the canyon. That was when Will Foreman stepped out from behind the boulders and called to him.

"Hold it right there, Arnold? You're covered."

For a along moment the outlaw sat like a statue aboard his mount, then slowly he turned to face Will Foreman.

"That's some lucky star followin' you around," he said through thick lips. "I'll never know how I managed to miss you last night."

"You jest ain't much good with a long gun, I reckon."

Will's Winchester .73 was pointing straight at Arnold's chest, finger on the trigger, hands rock-steady.

"Well ain't you gonna kill me after all the trouble you've been takin'?"

"I'm takin' you in, Arnold. Reckon there'll be a nice stretch o' hemp awaitin' that thick neck o' yours back in Denver, an' I'll be there to watch you swing."

The thick lips curled in contempt. "You think you can get me all the way back to Denver? You'll never make it."

"What's t'stop me?"

"I could draw on you right now. I'm good, so why don't you forget all about me an' just take Randolph to show you ain't been wastin' your time? Ain't no sense in you gettin' yourself killed tryin' to take me in."

Will had to acknowledge a grudging respect for the man's gall. No matter how fast Arnold might be on the draw he could not really fancy his chances against a man with a rifle pointing at his chest.

"I'm takin' you in, dead or alive, if you fancy your chance pullin' that forty-five. You'd be dead afore your gun clears leather."

They stared at each other in a long, nail-biting silence, until Will said, "Unbuckle your gun-belt an' toss it this way."

Will could recognize the signs as

Arnold weighed his chances, and knew the moment when he had won the first round in the battle of wills. Arnold reached with his left hand to release the buckle of his gun-belt, but even as he did so his other hand swept low to bring his gun up and out of its holster. Will shot him in the shoulder, spinning him round and tumbling him from the saddle as his horse reared in alarm. He hit the ground with enough force to knock all the wind out of his lungs.

He lay prone for more than a minute, clutching his shoulder. Will moved closer and watched the blood seeping through Arnold's fingers.

"Now ain't that tough, Arnold. You ain't dead after all; jest wounded. I hope it hurts."

With a snarl of fury Arnold scrambled to his knees and tried to pick up his fallen gun with a bloodied hand. Will dropped his rifle and fisted his Colt .44 in one smooth, swift action, and sent a bullet within inches of Arnold's forty-five. It was enough to temper

Arnold's fury with fright. Life was still precious, even with a bullet-hole in his left shoulder. He grimaced with pain and clutched at the wound again.

"Two hundred yards south you'll find my horse an' Keith Jackson's. Start walkin'."

Arnold's horse followed him without any instruction as he began walking, his decision already made to take the first opportunity to escape.

★ ★ ★

Hands manacled behind his back, in spite of the hole in his shoulder where Will Foreman's rifle-bullet had ploughed straight through, Eddie Arnold smirked with satisfaction as he watched Will examine Keith Jackson's wound.

"You really think you can get him back to Denver alive? He'll never make it."

Will turned furiously and snapped back, "I'd suggest you pray that he does, only I don't figure you've had any practice!"

"You can pray as much as you like, smart-ass, your ole man ain't ever gonna see Denver again."

Will threw away the blood-soaked plug that Jackson had used the night before and gave him some clean, white linen to stem the flow of bleeding that had started up again. He allowed the old man to do it himself because he was fearful of hurting him.

"He could be right, Will," Jackson whispered, his voice barely audible.

"Don't you even think it, Mr Jackson. I'll get you to a doctor if it's the last thing I do."

"If it comes to last things, shoot that sadist first."

Will took out his knife and cut two long lengths from young pines that had died from root rot. He fashioned a travois and fixed it to Randolph Carter's saddle, then led the horse back to collect the body.

Returning to Jackson he pulled out

a smile. "Can you stand up if I help you?"

It was a slow and painful procedure for the ageing Jackson to be helped to his feet and into the saddle of his buckskin.

"You lead the way, Mr Jackson. I'll get Arnold mounted an' follow at the rear. Call out if you need to stop for a break."

At first Arnold refused even to attempt to get on his horse, but when Will threatened him with a gun-barrel across his bulbous nose he agreed to co-operate, with Will giving him a heave to compensate for the manacled hands.

"Take these things off!" Arnold snapped irritably. "I can't ride with no hands!"

"You'd better, or you'll end up bruised all over. This ground is mighty hard an' the drop from your saddle is no easy fall. You could end up bustin' that other shoulder."

"I'll kill you for this!"

Will smiled at the empty threat.

Picking up the rope he had attached to the bridle of the dappled grey, he climbed aboard his own horse and set off in the rear.

Progress was made at a sedate walking pace, with the wounded Keith Jackson hanging on to his saddle-horn to stay aboard his horse, grimly fighting the pain and the nausea. Even killing Randolph Carter seemed poor compensation for the damage Carter had inflicted on him.

They rode for three hours, until Will noticed Jackson sway in the saddle. He called a halt and helped the old man down. Gathering wood, he built a fire and boiled coffee. The hot drink helped to revive Jackson's flagging energy, and even Eddie Arnold was silenced by the pain in his own body. He drank greedily as Will Foreman held a tin mug to his lips.

"This the first time you've been shot?"

Arnold snarled, "No, it ain't! Takes more'n one bullet to finish me off!"

"Next time I'll shoot you plumb centre, then we'll see."

He walked away before Arnold could respond.

A half-hour later they were saddle-borne again, with Will Foreman having grown increasingly anxious about his partner. Jackson needed a doctor real bad.

* * *

His bulging eyes blazing with pain and fury, Eddie Arnold yelled at Will, "Take these damned manacles off o' me, will you! My arms have gone dead!"

Will had selected their camp for the night and settled Keith Jackson against the bole of a pine before Arnold consented to dismount.

"Shut your fat mouth, Arnold. Your arms will never be as dead as that postmaster's you killed on the train — not 'til they hang you. Scum like you make me want to puke!"

"An' what gives you the right to talk that way to me? You tryin' to tell me you never killed a man?"

"I never tried robbin' a train!"

"Chicken, huh?"

Will walked towards him, eyes blazing. "Chicken? Is that what you call a man who tries to live a decent life? Men like you an' that gang you rode with reap nothin' but destruction wherever you go, leavin' pain an' misery in your wake. All you think about is gettin' money to satisfy your lust for whiskey an' women! Men like you ain't fit t'live!"

Had there been any expression in Arnold's cold eyes, the drooping lids would have covered it. Probably the only emotions he ever knew were lust and hate, Will concluded as he stomped back to attend to Jackson.

"Don't waste your anger on him, Will."

Will ignored the admonition. "I'll get you your blankets, Mr Jackson."

He managed to entice the old man

to eat a little after a fire had been built and coffee boiled again. Eddie Arnold was too proud to ask for food or drink and waited in silence until after Will had eaten himself. Only then did the prisoner get fed.

"Tell me somethin', Arnold . . . how long have you known we were on your trail?"

"About a week. When we couldn't lose you we decided to lure you into that canyon. Figured you'd be sittin' ducks, only we weren't sure you were Pinkerton men. You could've been bounty hunters for all we knew."

"Either way, you underestimated us."

Grudgingly Arnold conceded, "Looks that way."

"You've lost a lot o' blood. I ain't sure you'll make that hangman's rope after all. You got any kin?"

"None you need notify, only don't make any bets. Like I told you, it takes more than one bullet to kill me. Took more'n one to kill Randolph it seems."

"Yeah. Must've been a lot o' gunsmoke in the canyon last night. Was that when you quit tryin' t'kill me an' went lookin'?"

"Yeah. Only I figured it was the ole man who'd saddled a cloud while we were up there. Who is that ole man, anyway?"

"Keith Jackson. He's a survivor. Ain't a bettin' man alive who'd have gambled on him livin' half this long."

"You mean . . . "

"I mean he's killed or captured more lawbreakers than any sheriff or marshal who ever wore a badge. He's Pinkerton's oldest operative an' he ain't even thought o' quittin'."

"I reckon he's thinkin' about it now."

Will had no intention of admitting it, but he guessed Eddie Arnold was right for once. It would take all Jackson's grit and will-power to stay alive until a doctor could be found to remove the bullet lodged close to his spine.

4

ALL three men spent a restless night. Eddie Arnold's left shoulder caused him more pain than he would have openly admitted to Will Foreman, while Will himself was disturbed several times by Keith Jackson's spasmodic moaning and the worry about his partner. As the old man opened his eyes in the light of a new day he favoured Will with a wan smile of encouragement, but the younger man was not fooled. Jackson was hurting badly and he must have known there was a strong possibility of infection setting in before Will could get him to a doctor. To Will the danger was grimly obvious, and that worried him.

They wasted no time and as soon as Will had doused the fire after a meagre breakfast, he helped both men into their saddles. The procession moved off as of yesterday, with Jackson in the lead. Heading for lower ground, by midmorning they were down amongst the lower reaches. Under an azure-blue sky, his coat rolled and tied behind the cantle once more, Will found his spirits lifted by the warm sun. Even Keith Jackson grew more optimistic when Will called their first halt.

"Time for you to rest awhile, Mr Jackson," he told the old man when he hastened his roan alongside.

"I'm all right, Will. Don't stop for me."

"Sorry, Mr Jackson, but I'm givin' the orders now. No sense in overtaxin' yourself. You'll ride better after some rest. I'll fix you some hot coffee."

When he took Eddie Arnold's tin mug to him, filled with the hot liquid, the outlaw asked him to unshackle his hands.

"I'll hold it for you while you drink, same as before."

Obscenities flowed from Arnold's mouth like the torrent of a flash flood.

Will understood his frustration and the stiffness that must have numbed his arms and shoulders, while at the same time the hole in his left shoulder probably felt as if it was on fire. Arnold must have been suffering to reach the point when pride in his imperviousness to pain had dropped so low that he could admit it. Will Foreman felt no sympathy for him, remembering what he and his gang had done in the execution of train robbery. A badly wounded conductor and a dead postmaster were just two of the casualties of the gang's determination to rob the express car of sixty thousand dollars. It was their misfortune that Pinkerton agents were on that train and got into the fight.

"Well . . . why don't you say something?"

"I was givin' your mouth a chance to get tired," Will replied with glee.

In his rage Arnold chinned the tin mug out of Will's grasp when it was held up to his lips.

"You'll wish you hadn't done that afore I light another fire."

Will walked away with a warm glow sustaining him. Eddie Arnold was suffering and his bad-tempered outburst would make him suffer even more. Hot sun can soon dehydrate a man, especially a wounded one.

"Ready to go on, Mr Jackson?" Will queried after they had rested for an hour.

"We'd best travel as far as we can today, Will. Don't reckon I'll be in very good shape by tomorrow."

The admission was a reminder to Will that time was running against them. The need of a doctor for Jackson was growing more urgent.

"How far d'you think we are from the railroad, Mr Jackson?"

"Thirty miles or so. Maybe more to a depot."

"I reckon the engineer would stop his train for an emergency. Let's get goin'."

Will ignored Eddie Arnold's belligerent

protest with an equanimity he had not known he possessed, knowing the outlaw would realize he needed a doctor's help the same as Keith Jackson. His wound was clean, with the bullet having passed right through him, but he must have known it could turn septic without proper treatment. Grumbling the whole time, he nevertheless allowed Will to heave him aboard his horse.

In the early afternoon they came to a creek with clear water tumbling over the rocks, making them sparkle like diamonds under the blaze of sun. He let the horses drink and replenished the water bottles.

Green slopes led up to pines and spruce in the foothills. Away to the east, Will knew there was open prairie and the railroad that passed through Castle Rock. There was no way they could make it before sundown. Neither did he know how frequently the trains ran between Colorado Springs and Denver, or at what times they were due to stop at Castle Rock.

He drank from the crystal-clear water and gave a cupful to Jackson, aware that he was only staying in the saddle by sheer will-power, riding from memory and long experience.

A storm racing in from the west hit them late in the day and Will had a struggle to get Jackson's slicker around him. Eddie Arnold simply got wet, but the storm soon passed and his clothing steamed under the late sunshine. It did nothing to ease his temper.

Calling a halt in a treeless waste as daylight faded, Will was thankful that Jackson had reminded him he would need to gather kindling for a fire before they left the pine-covered slopes of the mountains, Now he went to the travois that Randolph Carter's dappled grey had been pulling since yesterday morning and collected his supply of timber. The corpse on the travois had begun to smell and Will released the horse and ground-picketed him some fifty yards away. Carter's body could be left in Castle Rock for burial once Will had reported to the town marshal or the county sheriff, whichever it might be.

Eddie Arnold was too pain-racked and weary to offer any trouble and Will decided he could take off the manacles and let the outlaw feed himself and hold his own tin mug for drinking. Arnold's coat was stained dark with dried blood back and front, testimony to the weakness that had enveloped him. Will would be relieved to hand him over to the local peace officer.

Keith Jackson was now too weak to hold his own tin mug and Will had to encourage him to sip the hot coffee in the hope of renewing some of his lost energy. A feeble shake of the head was all it needed to tell Will the old man was not interested in food.

He was tempted to saddle up again and ride to the town for help, but he feared that in the darkness he could so easily ride in the wrong direction and miss the town completely. He needed the sun as a compass and clear daylight before taking any more risks. Determined to ride at dawn, he settled the old man, satisfied himself that Eddie Arnold had already fallen asleep, then unfurled his own bedroll.

★ ★ ★

It was the click of a rifle hammer on an empty chamber that woke him. He sat up and watched Eddie Arnold working the lever feverishly in bitter frustration. Why the hell had he not checked the gun when he took it from Randolph Carter's saddle-pouch with the intention of killing his captor? Even Arnold himself recognized the answer. He had been afraid that breaking open the gun would have made just enough noise to alert Will Foreman. It was no consolation.

Will grinned gleefully as he got to his feet. "You must be a damned fool if you thought I'd let you sleep without those manacles an' then leave a loaded gun around for you to get your hands on."

"*Damn you!*" Arnold screamed, reversing the gun with the aim of clubbing Will with the butt.

"Drop it!"

Arnold stared at the Colt .44 that suddenly appeared in Will Foreman's right hand, and let out a sound that was a mingle of snarl and whine. He dropped the rifle and turned away at a run. Will laughed. He knew that Arnold, with all the blood he had lost, would not get far.

It came as no surprise to see that Arnold had already saddled his horse for a getaway, but when the outlaw climbed into the saddle in obvious pain, then galloped away, Will saddled his own roan without hurrying, then rode after the fugitive.

When he came within striking distance some twenty minutes later, Will uncoiled his lariat as he rode, whirled it a dozen times, then aimed the loop at the head of the horse in front. Eddie Arnold was crouched precariously over his horse's withers and he tumbled out of the saddle with a cry of agony when it was brought to a halt, straining against the rope around its neck. The other end of the lariat was firmly around Will Foreman's saddle-horn.

Shortening the rope as his own horse moved closer, Will looked into those large, bulging eyes blazing with fury and said, "I didn't risk gettin' killed on that mountain to let you get away now, Eddie. Like I told you afore, I aim t'see you hang."

Arnold climbed painfully to his feet. "You gonna make me walk back to that camp?"

"No, Eddie, you can ride, only remember this . . . next time it won't be this rope. You make one more attempt to ride off an' I'll put another bullet into you, straight through the heart. You're a long time dead, Eddie."

In view of what he had told Arnold moments earlier it seemed an odd thing to say, but then he knew that as long as the outlaw lived, hope would linger in his mind.

Will released the loop from around the horse's neck as Arnold climbed painfully back into the saddle. Then before the outlaw realized what was happening, Will dropped the rope over his head, pinning his arms by his sides as the loop was swiftly tightened.

"Reckon I'd best manacle you again, then I can forget about you gettin' reckless."

Having his hands manacled behind his back yet again was the final humiliation for the outlaw. He rode alongside Will, back to Keith Jackson, in sullen silence.

5

KEITH JACKSON'S eyes were still closed when Will Foreman picked up the remaining firewood and, wanting to give the old man as much rest as he could, Will did not disturb him until he had a steaming mug ready to offer.

"Mr Jackson."

There was a long silence before Jackson breathed out Will's name. He did not open his eyes and Will's concern deepened. He touched Jackson's forehead, shiny with perspiration. It was hot and Will knew instantly that fever had set in. Getting the wounded veteran back to civilization was imperative.

Jackson opened his eyes. "I'm too sick to ride, Will."

"I know. Don't worry, I'll put you on the travois. Pity about Carter, but you're more important. Try an' take a few sips. Don't want you gettin' dehydrated."

Feebly Jackson took one sip at a time, with a long break between each one. Will contained his impatience to get going, making Eddie Arnold wait for his sustenance. If the outlaw offered any show of belligerence at having his hands manacled and being served by Will, then he would go without, Will decided, half hoping Arnold's irritation would burst out again in another torrent of abuse. Anything that would save time would lessen Will's apprehension.

Chasing after the escaping outlaw had eaten into the early morning, but even so, Will hoped to make Castle Rock before noon. He estimated they were no more than ten miles from the town and he prayed there would be a doctor living there. It was a town he had never visited.

Although he seldom wore spurs, Will always carried an old pair of the work variety, with fairly blunt rowels, in his saddle-bags. He used one of them to loosen an area of soft earth, grave-size, and clawed away with his hands to make a hole big enough to take Randolph Carter's body. It was tedious and exhausting work and of necessity a shallow grave, but if anybody took enough interest to give the dead outlaw a more dignified burial in the coming days, then the ashes from the fires Will had fashioned would be a marker for finding the spot. Jackson would endure an uncomfortable ride on the travois, but all he had to do was lie there. Both he and Will knew he could never have sat a saddle for ten miles.

* * *

The luxury of sleeping in a hotel bed should have refreshed the young Pinkerton man, yet all the tossing and turning he had done, frequently waking and wondering if Keith Jackson would survive, left him feeling listless and dispirited as he sat down to breakfast. He wondered what response would be forthcoming from the Chicago office to the telegraph he had sent the day before. He was not entirely sure if his choice of words had been quite right.

JACKSON SERIOUSLY WOUNDED STOP CARTER DEAD ARNOLD ARRESTED STOP AWAIT INSTRUCTIONS STOP

Had he said enough? Bearing in mind the confidential nature of the Pinkerton Detective Agency's work, he had told only the minimum. If they wanted more, then they would have to ask for it.

Somehow he did not think they would be too worried about losing Keith Jackson's services; they must have known he was not going to go on working forever. The man was fifty-eight years old and had aged physically during the seven years Will had been siding him. It was only his experience and guile that had allowed him to remain active for so long.

Not that Pinkertons were an unfeeling

family, and Will knew that Mr Allan Pinkerton would be distressed to learn of the critical condition Keith Jackson was in. It would not surprise Will in the least if the head of the organization decided to come out and visit the wounded man in person, or at least send one of his sons to see what could be done to alleviate Jackson's suffering. Dr Larner offered no hope of complete recovery after he removed the bullet from Jackson's body. It had been an extremely difficult task and before making any attempt to operate he had warned both Will and the patient that he was insufficiently experienced for such surgery.

"Suppose you don't . . . operate, Doc?" Jackson had whispered through his pain and fever.

"You'll die, Mr Jackson."

Will recognized the absolute honesty of the doctor and in no way felt inclined to chastise him for its brutal candour.

"Then . . . get on . . . with it."

Will ate his breakfast listlessly. Keith Jackson had been as good as a father to him for more than seven years and the possibility of the old man dying was a disturbing thought. Whatever happened, Will decided, it was time to quit chasing robbers and get back to his first love, breaking horses. How easy or difficult it would be to get a bronc-busting job he had no idea. After all those years with Jackson he was out of touch with the life of ranching.

He wiped his mouth, got up from the table and headed for the doctor's house.

Gabriel Larner greeted him with a sombre face. It alarmed Will Foreman as he was invited inside.

"Is he . . . ?" Will faltered in his query.

"He's holding his own at the moment, but the fever is high and you should prepare yourself for the worst."

"Can I see him?"

"If you wish, but I must warn you that he won't know you're there. When

I looked in on him a few minutes ago he was in delirium."

The doctor's wife looked up as the two men entered the room. She had a cold compress held against the patient's forehead and her eyes were grave. Will speculated on how much contact she had known with men who might die, in spite of what her husband might be able to do.

She was a small woman whose black hair was already sprinkled with a few grey strands. Like her balding husband, she was well past her fortieth summer.

Will stared down at the lined face in need of a shave. The moustache was almost white now, where it had only been flecked with grey when Jackson had persuaded the sheriff in Abilene all those years ago that Will was innocent of unlawful killing. Those piercing grey eyes that had made such an impression on the young Will Foreman were closed and Will could not stem the fear that they might never open again.

"Would you like to sit with him,

Mr Foreman?" the doctor's wife asked. "This compress needs squeezing out and dipping into the cold water every few minutes. Could you do that for me, while I get on with some chores?"

After a momentary hesitation, Will answered, "Sure, Mrs Larner, I'd be glad to."

"I have to go out, Mr Foreman," Gabriel Larner told him. "I'll be back as soon as I can, although there is nothing more I can do for him. Only God can help him now."

Will sat with Jackson for an hour, then Mrs Larner came in to take over.

"There's nothing you can do for him now, Mr Foreman. If you have other business to attend to . . . ?"

Will cogitated for several heartbeats, totally lost in a situation he had thought could never happen, and wondered what he might do while he waited for Jackson either to die or to recover.

"I guess I'd best see to the horses," he announced after a while.

The horses were safely lodged in the livery stables, including those of Eddie Arnold and Randolph Carter. Carter's horse would be sold to pay the stable owner, any residue going to the town funds, but Will's roan and Jackson's buckskin would need exercising. It would be something to do while he awaited instructions from Chicago.

* * *

Keith Jackson wavered between life and death for more than a week, fighting a tougher battle than any he had encountered in his years of hunting down outlaws.

Towards the end of the eighth day the fever began to subside and his temperature slowly returned to normal. It had been a long struggle for Gabriel Larner as well as his patient, and when the doctor imparted the good news to Will Foreman they both smiled with immense relief.

"I allus said that old man was immortal," Will said.

The doctor took a more sober view. "Don't get too optimistic, Will. He's an old man and he'll never be the same as he was before. His days hunting outlaws are over."

"Yeah. I guess I knew that, Doc. An'so are mine. Mr Jackson has been like a father t'me."

Now twenty-three years old, it suddenly occurred to Will that he had never once addressed the old man by his forename, always formally giving him his title with the respect he had been taught to offer older men. It was a measure of the admiration Keith Jackson had inspired in his young partner. Will knew it would never change. His mentor would always remain 'Mr Jackson'.

The doctor cut into his reverie. "What will you do, Will?"

"I'll go back to wranglin', but right now I guess I'd best send a wire to Mr Pinkerton. What do I tell him, Doc?"

"Best choose your words carefully. The patient could have a relapse at any time. He's not out of the wood yet."

"Improving?" Will suggested.

"That should cover it."

★ ★ ★

It was arranged by the Pinkerton Detective Agency that Keith Jackson should be transported to a nursing home in the mountains as soon as he was fit to travel. Will Foreman had watched the steady improvement the old man made each day with relief and joy. If Jackson had died, Will knew he would have felt devastated.

On the forty-third day after the gunsmoke had cleared in that canyon, Will Foreman accompanied Jackson to the nursing home. Once settled in his clean white sheets, Jackson submitted to the weariness the journey had brought upon him.

"Come and see me tomorrow, Will, and we'll talk."

"Sure thing, Mr Jackson. You get some sleep now."

* * *

Will sat beside Jackson's bed the next day and noticed how haggard the old man had become. He looked even older than he really was.

"I guess this is the end, Will."

"The end, Mr Jackson?"

Will's response was a pretence at naïvety. Both men had known for some weeks their criminal-chasing partnership had ended in that canyon and both of them had deliberately refused to face up to it. The bond between them was even stronger than either of them realized.

"You know what I mean, Will. I'm finished."

"Aw, come on, Mr Jackson! There's plenty o' life in you yet."

"No, Will. I may last a while, may even get out of this place in time, but my riding days are over. The question is, what about you?"

Will played with his hat, something he often did in times of nervousness. "I told Mr Pinkerton I was about ready to quit."

"He must have been disappointed. Is that what you really want?"

Will gave out a nervous laugh. "Wouldn't be the same without you, Mr Jackson."

"The boss will be sorry to lose you. You've become a good operative."

"That was never what I really wanted, although I've enjoyed siding you. I've learned a lot alongside you, especially about the art of survival." Another short laugh. "Reckon I'm even more patient than I used to be."

Just for a moment there was a spark of pleasure in the old grey eyes. "You're a better shot than you used to be."

"Yeah. I don't waste lead these days."

"So what now, Will?"

"I'll get me a job on a ranch some place, wranglin' if I can. It's what my daddy trained me for, ever since I was a little colt."

Jackson smiled at the analogy. He knew Will had never been in touch with his folks in all the years they had been together and he had never pried into the reason. Now he felt the desire to know.

"You never talked about why you left Texas, Will."

"I killed a man back home, Mr Jackson."

The confession was out before Will realized he might have put the Pinkerton man under an obligation he did not want.

"Figured it might be something like that, but don't you ever wonder how your folks are?"

"All the time, though I try not to think about it."

"I reckon you've caused them a lot of heartache while you've been with me."

"I guess so, but they'll understand why I've never been in touch. The warrant for my arrest must still be in force. Don't reckon they'd want me to hang."

"Were you that guilty?"

"No, only I'd have a hard time provin' it."

Will told him about the vicious brute who had been using a bull-whip on a horse and how, when Will protested, that same whip had been wrapped around Will's throat, choking the life out of him. "I had to kill him, Mr Jackson. He was stranglin' me."

"I always wondered. Figured you'd tell me in your own good time if you wanted me to know."

There was something else Will wanted to impart to his mentor and he knew it would please him.

"I got a message from Chicago this mornin'," he opened tentatively.

"And?"

"Eddie Arnold's trial is fixed for next week. I'm called to give evidence of arrest. I'll have t'leave in the mornin', Mr Jackson."

"You'll come back and give me the news?"

"I will. I'm gonna enjoy seein' that varmint hang."

6

KEITH JACKSON already knew the trial verdict before Will got back to see him.

"I read the account in the newspapers, Will. Arnold must have gotten himself a good lawyer."

"Yeah, but he ain't gonna like bein' locked up for the next ten years."

"I gathered that from the threats he made."

Will laughed harshly. "He'll've forgotten all about that ten years from now."

"I wouldn't be too sure about that. He might even escape in a few months, so I suggest you keep your eyes on the newspapers. Prison guards can be bribed, let me remind you."

"I told you, Mr Jackson, I'm gonna lose m'self on a ranch some place."

The reminder cast a shadow over

Jackson's eyes. "Decided where?"

"Some place not too far away. I'd like to visit as much as I can."

"Don't you worry about me, son. You don't owe me a thing."

"That ain't so. Without you I coulda been dead by now."

"Call it even then. If it hadn't been for you, I'd have died in that canyon."

A wide smile showed strong white teeth. "We've been a good team, ain't we?"

"Without you, Will, I'd have had to retire years ago, I reckon."

"Not you, Mr Jackson. You'd have died o' boredom."

The old grey eyes opened fractionally more than their normal minimum. "Don't intend to do that, Will. I'm going to catch up on all those books I never managed to read."

Will looked around at some of the other patients. "You might even find enough hands in here for a poker session."

"Could be."

Will stayed for an hour, satisfied with the progress Keith Jackson had made during his absence, assuring him he would pay him another visit within the next few weeks, depending on how he fared in his search for work.

★ ★ ★

David Clay contemplated him with unconcealed curiosity as Will Foreman spoke of his background. Will acknowledged his lack of recent experience in capturing and breaking wild horses. Clay revealed that he ran a fair-sized herd of cattle, but was also a horse trader who did most of his own breaking. Now in his late forties, he was finding the bruises did not heal quickly enough and in Will Foreman he saw potential salvation.

"Just one thing, Foreman . . . you give me your word you're not still working for Pinkerton's?"

"You have my word on it, Mr Clay. My partner got shot real bad. I didn't wanna go on without him."

"All right. We'll see how we get along for a month. If I'm satisfied, and you want to stay . . . "

"Fair enough, only I'd like to pay a visit afore we make it permanent."

"Sick visiting?"

"Right."

"I guess we can work something out."

"Thanks, Mr Clay."

"My boys should be back for supper soon. My ramrod is a feller named Pete Taylor. He'll find you a spare bunk. Meantime, I'll show you a bronc that needs bustin'. I'll warn you now, he's a mean one, and with you being out of practice, you might as well see what you can do with him for an hour."

Will knew the rancher was giving him a tough test to see how much guts he had. It came as no surprise. Any other boss would have made his return to bronc-busting tough, just to see what he was made of, but now the stomach nerves began to play up.

Did he still have his touch? Would his nerve hold after he'd been thrown a few times?

He was about to find out.

★ ★ ★

Cowboys hungry for supper were diverted to the bronc-busting corral when they saw their boss watching what was going on inside. They had missed the first half-hour of Will Foreman's re-entry into the wrangling game, when he had spent time letting the near-black stallion get used to his presence in the enclosure, talking softly to him, trying to ease the fear he had of his enemy — man. It was man who had robbed him of his freedom and he resented that with a fierce determination not to be tamed. Will had been taught by his father that it was always wise to geld a wild horse before you tried to break him, but to suggest that to David Clay on first acquaintance might have been construed as fear on his part. He recalled having been given the challenge of breaking a stallion a few days before his sixteenth birthday and the memory of his final victory on that occasion gave him encouragement now.

David Clay's parting shot before Will had climbed between the corral poles was designed to minimize the task he faced, but it would also diminish Will's accomplishment, whatever that might be. "At least I've gotten a saddle on him for you."

Conscious of the audience around him, Will felt himself under even more pressure.

Bucking and plunging, the bronc jogged his violent way around the enclosure, with Will bracing and alternately relaxing his body to take the strain of rise and fall. If he got out of this first battle with no bones broken he would consider he had won the skirmish. Aching muscles he had long accepted as the price a wrangler had to put up with for his monthly pay-packet. They were the only medals a man could earn in this kind of war, he recalled his father telling him, but the satisfaction of taming a wild horse gave a man a sense of pride he could find no other way.

The cook played his less-than musical tune on the triangle to call the men to supper, much to Will's relief.

David Clay called out to him, "That's enough for now, Will. Give your muscles a rest until morning."

Will threw himself out of the saddle and landed neatly on his feet, fully aware the cook had saved him from what might have proved a nasty fall. The stallion had been on the verge of winning a few points. He ducked between the poles to be introduced to the Clay ramrod. The two men shook hands with a simultaneous 'Howdy'.

In the cookhouse a large table was surrounded by bench seats and, with Will and Pete Taylor bringing up the rear, the foreman introduced each man to the new wrangler. Taylor had removed his hat to reveal receding dark hair. He seemed an amiable enough man, with dark brown, bright eyes that hinted at an easy-going nature, but Will decided he would have looked better without the week's growth of stubble on face and chin.

The clatter of eating-irons and hard-working jaws were death to conversation, but the meal was soon over and the banter of cowboys wearied by a day's work began. Will Foreman was neither ignored nor included in the chatter, but every man at one time or another slanted glances his way, each wanting to know something about him, yet observing the unwritten code that you did not ask a man about his past. If he wanted to impart information about himself that was up to him.

Gradually Will began to put names to faces for future use, otherwise he was content to listen to the joshing that always went on amongst men familiar with each other.

In the bunkhouse he was allotted a bunk, then invited to participate in a game of poker. Now that he had quit the Pinkerton Agency he intended to play card games as little as possible, but here in new surroundings, amongst men who were for the time being strangers, it would be policy to ingratiate himself until he had been accepted as one of them. He was thankful to find there was no card-sharp amongst them and he lost very little.

His new surroundings and an unfamiliar bunk were not conducive to easy sleeping and in the morning he awoke with muscles stiffened by unaccustomed activity the day before. It was something he would soon get used to again and he looked forward to getting back working with horses.

By the end of the day he was bruised and aching, but the battle with the stallion had gone in his favour by the time the cook rattled his triangle again, and David Clay seemed satisfied with his new wrangler.

"You've done well today, Will. After

supper we'll cut that black, then leave him to heal for a day or two. I guess he'll be more amenable after that. Tomorrow we'll go riding. See if we can pick us up a few more wild ones."

"You have any trouble findin' horses now, boss?"

"Not so far. Far as I know there's no other rancher around for miles who doesn't prefer his *remuda* already broke, so I've gotten the business to myself. Those canyons still hold a few strong stallions with their mares and I've never found it too hard to pick out strong young 'uns. That black is the type I favour, so we'll see what we can find."

"You ever thought o' cuttin' them afore you start breakin' them, Mr Clay?"

Clay grinned. "I usually do, but every now and then I like to see if I can still break a full horse. I suppose it's just foolish pride. Lucky I picked on that black; helped me see you know your job. We'll get along, Will."

In spite of his aching muscles, Will was thankful to have stumbled on to the Clay ranch.

7

DAVID CLAY told the cook to put up enough grub for Will and himself to last four days, explaining to Will, "We don't want to have to come back until we've gotten what we want. It would be maddening if we found a herd and then didn't give ourselves time to cut out a few."

Clay's perception proved to be wise. They found no horses at all on the first day and made camp an hour before dark by a clear running creek. The rancher took the opportunity to get to know his new wrangler a little better, while Will did some probing of his own.

"This old partner of yours, Will . . . is he in that place up in the mountains?"

"He is. Gets mighty cold up there at nights, but the days are idyllic. He'll never be the same again, but at least he'll get good care with what's left for him in this life."

"You figure his days are numbered?"

The question made Will's throat tighten and his answer was slow in coming. "The medics told me to prepare for the worst. He could live a month or a coupla years, but his wound was a bad 'un. That first week was a constant battle for him to survive. He was delirious for days." Will was silent in reflection for long moments. "First time any man ever got the better of him."

"I guess you were close, huh?"

"I'd like to go on workin' for you, Mr Clay, but I'll need three or four days off every month, if we can come to terms with that?"

"Should be no problem, Will," Clay conceded, thinking that Keith Jackson would probably be called to that great ranch in the sky within a year.

"How long you been without a wrangler, Mr Clay?"

"Never hired one before, Will. You just happened along when I figured I needed help." He gave a short laugh. "I'm heading towards fifty. My body can't take the falls as well as it did a few years ago."

Silence dominated for a couple of minutes, then, "You never married, Mr Clay?"

"Oh, sure I did. Did none of the boys mention my wife and daughter are away on a trip?"

"No, they didn't."

"Well . . . they went to see my sister-in-law in Topeka. They should be back next week."

Idly Will Foreman wondered what David Clay's daughter was like and how old she might be. Clay himself was a handsome man for his age, with an abundance of greying hair and bright brown eyes, and if his wife matched his looks, then the daughter could well be something of a beauty.

He piled more wood on to the fire before they settled in their soogans.

Clay was soon breathing heavily in his sleep, and even Will Foreman's memories of other girls were quickly lost to drowsiness as distant coyotes wailed their calls on the night wind.

Slowly the fire died.

* * *

Nancy Clay had long, straight, corn-coloured hair reaching way below her shoulders. It shone like silk under the hot sun. She was obviously years younger than her husband, with fine bone-structure, laughing eyes and the shape of mouth that could send shivers of desire surging through much younger men. Full-breasted, her waist accentuated by the cut of her riding habit, eastern-style, she commanded attention, and Will blushed when he realized he had been staring at her.

"Nancy," David Clay began by way of introduction, "this is Will Foreman. I've hired him to share the bruises in this corral."

Will had been about to duck between the corral poles when Clay's call halted him.

"Hello, Will Foreman. Welcome to the Clay ranch."

Will doffed his hat and nodded. "Howdy, ma'am. Glad to be here."

She turned away and looked at the four horses in the corral. "Are these the new ones you brought back while we were away?" she asked her husband.

"They are. Like 'em?"

"Oh, yes. I like that chestnut. He's a handsome feller." Her head twisted to look back at Clay. "Pity you gelded him. He would have made a good stallion."

Clay laughed good-humouredly and turned to Will. "My wife thinks it would be better if I started breeding instead of heading off into the mountains every few weeks, Will. I keep telling her it's cheaper than feeding foals until they're old enough to be sold."

"I guess you're right about that."

The woman glanced from one to the

other. "And what about the risks you take? I keep telling my husband, Mr Foreman, it would be easier to break in young horses that have spent all their lives on the ranch, rather than risk getting his back broken with these wild ones. Don't you think that chestnut would have made a fine stud?"

"Yes, ma'am, he sure would," Will enthused, but then realized he might have said the wrong thing. He looked back at David Clay. "Sorry, boss, I guess I spoke out o' turn."

"No need to apologize, Will. When my wife asks a question she expects a straight answer. That's what you gave her."

Clay might not be willing to do exactly what his wife would have liked, but Will could see he would never entirely ignore her suggestions. He would lead her to believe that maybe one day he would act on her advice. The man clearly adored his much younger mate. Will wondered how he could bear to let her go off to Topeka for a month without him.

"Guess I'd best get to work."

"You do that, Will, then my wife will see we're not just reckless fools taking stupid risks."

Will climbed through the rails and concentrated on the job that had to be done.

"Now you watch, Nancy, and learn how a real horseman goes about breaking a bronc."

She watched for half an hour, then turned to Clay and whispered, "But he hasn't *done* anything!"

"Oh, yes, he has." Clay's voice was as quiet as that of his wife. "See how they accept him in the corral? He's not an intruder into their domain, he's the boss of the corral and *they know it*. They don't fear him any more.

"See how easily he got the hackamore on that chestnut? I never managed it in such a short time. He has enormous patience, and he's convinced me it pays in the long run. Once they've accepted him as a friend instead of an enemy, they won't fight him as much."

"You sure about that? Has he proved it?"

"Not yet, but I'm convinced he will."

Will had concentrated so hard on the horse with the shiny chestnut coat that it was not until he ducked out of the corral that he noticed a third spectator. Clay introduced them.

Henrietta Clay bore little resemblance to her mother. The mouth and chin were similar, but the eyes were brown and so was the hair, a shade almost as dark as Will Foreman's. The girl had it cut short, just below her ears. She was pretty, with a broad and friendly smile revealing even, white teeth, a picture of youthful innocence. Her slender body was in sharp contrast to her mother's mature beauty and Will wondered if the girl would ever be quite as alluring as her parent.

She blushed when Will flashed his teeth and gave her his undivided attention.

"Did you enjoy your trip, Miss Clay?"

"Yes . . . thank you."

"Go get yourself some coffee, Will," Clay said sharply. "You've earned it."

Will recognized his dismissal and ambled towards the cookhouse. He heard what he guessed was not intended for his ears. Nancy Clay's voice wafted to him on the breeze.

"Henrietta! Have you never seen a good-looking young man before? Your face is scarlet!"

A smile of pleasure touched Will Foreman's lips as he heard the girl's running feet heading back to the house.

★ ★ ★

The days were long and hard, but by the end of his first month in David Clay's employ, Will's body had attuned itself to the rigours his chosen work demanded of it. He had seen little of Henrietta Clay since their first meeting, but each time the girl rode out with her mother he noticed she cast a fleeting glance in his direction. Will chose to ignore the girl, mindful of the risks in getting on the wrong side of Clay's wife. The woman herself treated him cordially, often coming to the corral to watch him work.

"It's easy to see you love horses, Will," she told him after he had broken the three mustangs.

With a sense of mischief Will answered, "A man should treat a horse the same as he would a woman . . . with respect."

It was a heart-felt sentiment.

"And love?"

"Yes, ma'am, definitely with love. A horse responds to love much quicker than harsh treatment."

So does a woman, she wanted to say, but bridled her tongue as she remembered how her daughter had looked at this handsome young Texan. Her ambitions for Henrietta were set far higher than a bronc-buster, no matter how charming and respectful he might be. Tomorrow he would be gone for a few days and she could relax her vigilance. Henrietta had shown no interest in any of the other men her husband employed.

* * *

Impatient to visit with Keith Jackson, Will pushed the roan harder than he would normally have done on that first day.

He camped in the lower reaches that night with his mind on the years he had shared with Jackson in pursuit of the ungodly, but the face he saw as he closed his eyes was that of Henrietta Clay.

In the morning he saddled the roan as the sun broke over the mountains, keen to complete his journey.

Jackson greeted him with a hint of pleasure in those piercing eyes that never seemed to open fully. "You're looking good, Will."

"How are you, Mr Jackson?"

"Getting old, son."

Will laughed. "*You'll* never be old, Mr Jackson."

"Sit a spell and tell me your news."

For fifteen minutes Will talked almost non-stop, his joy in having found the work he wanted clearly evident to the old man. When he got around to mentioning Clay's wife and daughter, Jackson was moved to offer a warning.

"If that girl took a shine to you, Will, best tread softly. You don't want to lose the job now you've found what you want."

"Mr Jackson! D'you think I'm dumb?"

"No, Will, that you ain't. After more than seven years with me, you should have learned a bit of sense, but even you can be buffaloed by a pretty face, I reckon."

"Oh, that Henrietta is pretty all right, but if I was a dumb fool it'd be her mother I'd be makin' a play for. She's one helluva woman, Mr Jackson."

"But she ain't the one likely to encourage you."

"That's a fact."

The visit lasted two hours, then Will promised to return the next day before heading back to the Clay ranch. Had he known what awaited him outside he would not have sounded so cheerful.

8

THAT sixth sense he had developed during his years alongside Keith Jackson warned him that something was wrong as he walked to his horse. A tingling sensation down his spine was the signal that alerted him to the danger. When he turned and gazed around him there was only one man within his range of view. There was an indication in the way the man stood, his eyes fixed on Will, his left hand hovering near the holstered, pearl-handled gun. A man not as tall as Will, a cleft in his chin, mouth slightly open, as if he might have problems breathing only through his nose. He began to walk slowly towards Will Foreman.

Will started down the slope to meet him, wanting to get well wide of his horse, looking into glazed eyes.

"You must be Will Foreman."

Will wondered how he could be so sure. The man stopped twenty yards away.

"An' who might you be?"

"Anthony Newcombe. You and that old man in there . . . " He nodded towards the nursing home, " . . . killed my cousin."

"Your cousin?"

"Randolph Carter."

If Newcombe knew that much he probably also knew that it was Keith Jackson who had pumped the bullets into his cousin, so why had he not gone inside the home and finished off the old man?

"So you think killin' me will set things straight, huh?"

"You catch on quick."

Curiosity surfaced in Will's mind. "How did you know I was here?"

"I've waited two weeks for you to visit that old man. I was told you'd be sure to come soon. Had someone keep an eye on the place."

"An' after you've killed me, you aim to go in there an' finish off Mr Jackson."

"No need. He ain't gonna live long anyways."

Will wondered briefly how Newcombe had been getting his information, but he was more concerned about his own survival. He had never heard of any Anthony Newcombe with a reputation as a gunfighter, but this man was oozing self-confidence. If he was so well informed, how come he had not heard of Will's prowess with a Colt .44?

Maybe he had, and yet still fancied his chances. Will had heard that left-handed gunfighters were often very fast on the draw. He wondered how fast this one was. He did not want to find out.

"You wanna die tryin' to get revenge for that skunk Carter? He was never worth it."

"You've gotten it wrong, Foreman. *You're* the one who's gonna die."

Newcombe's fingers clutched his gun-butt and lifted it clear of leather, and in one swift, smooth motion it was levelled and spitting lead. Gun-thunder reverberated around the mountain as a wash of red ran down his face, but Will Foreman never saw the hinges of his knees slowly close as they sank to the ground and, mouth agape, Newcombe sprawled forward in a death-fall.

The force of Newcombe's shot plunging into his chest spun Will Foreman around and the stench of cordite filled his nostrils as another bullet ploughed its way into his fleshy thigh.

Still shot-sound echoed all around him. He could not understand it. Surely he had drawn and fired as fast as Newcombe and it was inconceivable that he had missed the gunman completely.

Just as suddenly as it had begun, the shooting ceased and shot-sound was replaced by the rattle of iron-shod hooves rapidly fading into the distance.

Rolling over and over, clutching at his wounded thigh, his own gun jerked out of his hand by the shock of bullets hitting him, he caught a glimpse of Anthony Newcombe lying quite still, as the lids came down over his own brown eyes, his brow furrowed by the burning pain of his wounds.

The tide of fortune was running low and he seemed powerless to halt it. He needed help. Blood was running between his fingers and he had the vague feeling he was leaking like a sieve. This was not the first time he had been shot, but previously he had only suffered superficial wounds; this time the damage was far more serious and he felt weakness consuming him.

Hands lifted him and carried him away and then the blackness descended, shutting out the pain.

★ ★ ★

Keith Jackson was sitting beside his bed, his face a mask. As Will's eyes focused to meet Jackson's steady gaze, he reflected how unemotional the old man always seemed, even after he had been gut-shot in that canyon. It was an example to Will not to allow Jackson to see the extent of his own pain and anguish.

"How does it feel, son?"

"Takes more'n a coupla bullets to kill me, Mr Jackson."

"You stopped more than a couple, Will. Doc says you looked like a colander after they gotten the clothes off of you."

"I don't get it, Mr Jackson. That Newcombe was as still as death the last time I saw him."

"It weren't just him, Will. He'd gotten himself some help. I guess once they saw Newcombe go down they figured it was up to them to finish you off. Almost succeeded, too."

Will's voice betrayed his anxiety. "Am I hurt bad?"

"Doc says if you'd been my age you wouldn't have survived, but you're young. He gives you a fighting chance."

"Did I ever tell you you're a real Job's comforter, Mr Jackson?"

"That you did, Will, I seem to recall."

Brief remarks punctuated by long silences allowed Will to assess the damage that had been inflicted on his young body, and slowly anger mingled with his pain. He recognized that the fire of life had been at its lowest ebb before the effects of the ether the doctor had administered wore off, and now the hunger to go and get even with the men who had been intent on killing him burned into his brain.

"Who were they, Mr Jackson?"

"This is not the time to be worrying about that, son. You'll be safe here for quite a spell. Don't you fret. I sent a telegraph to Chicago. You just concentrate on getting well again."

Will wondered if the Pinkerton Detective Agency would do anything about the attack on him, or merely sympathize and forget it. After all, he was no longer one of their employees, so it was most unlikely they would spare men to hunt down the gunmen when they were always short of operatives to meet their obligations. What concerned Will far more was the knowledge that he had made a promise to David Clay he was now unable to keep.

"Could you write a letter for me, Mr Jackson?"

★ ★ ★

"I don't understand it," David Clay told his wife. "Something must have happened to him. He should've been back a week ago."

Nancy Clay answered, "You don't think you misjudged him?"

This was not the first time they had discussed Will Foreman's failure to return. Nancy Clay had been secretly delighted, gladdened by the prospect of her daughter being freed from a disastrous infatuation, only too aware that parental opposition to a girl's wishes simply made them grow unreasonably stronger. Each time his name had been mentioned she had done her best to diminish her husband's faith in his new wrangler.

Clay retorted sharply, "No, I don't! I know men, and I'm certain Will would not break his word without a darned good reason." He thrust his hands deeper into his pockets, frowning. Then, his mind made up, he announced, "I'm going to find him. Expect me when you see me."

Henrietta Clay had been unable to get the image of the handsome Will Foreman's smile out of her mind, and at her father's pronouncement she rose from the table, having drained her coffee cup, and asked, "Can I come with you, Daddy?"

"What for?"

"I'm bored and I would be company for you."

Clay looked at his wife to get her reaction to their daughter's suggestion. The woman shrugged confidently. "Let her go with you. It will be an experience for her."

He guessed what his wife was thinking. She expected them to discover that Will Foreman had found something more to his liking and she wanted her daughter to become thoroughly disillusioned about the young Texan. Clay was convinced that he was right and his wife wrong, but he kept the thought to himself.

He turned to his daughter. "Pack up enough food to last us for a week. I'll saddle the horses."

★ ★ ★

The man standing beside Will's bed was tall and broad, dressed in a city suit. Will decided it didn't go with his general appearance. The horns of his huge moustache stretched right across his face and his smile was wide. An enormous hand lifted the tall stetson from his bald head.

"Mind if I sit down, young feller?"

96

"Help yourself." They contemplated each other for a dozen heartbeats, until Will asked, "Who are you?"

"Nigel Kent. I guess I owe you."

"How come?"

The smile had disappeared and now the man looked contrite. There was something troubling him and Will guessed he was choosing his words carefully in the short pause.

"I guess I'm responsible for you getting shot. You see, I talked to two fellers in town about Mr Jackson being up here." He nodded towards another patient further down the room. "Alastair Fox down there is a friend of mine. I've been visiting for quite a spell."

Will could guess the rest.

The two men Kent had become friendly with in the saloon in town had talked about the trial of Eddie Arnold, reported in the newspapers, and Kent had revealed that Keith Jackson, one of the men responsible for the outlaw's capture, was convalescing close by.

Will's name had cropped up in the conversation and Kent had let it slip that he was expected to visit Jackson soon. The men had simply waited for Will to return, then set up the ambush.

"So you see, young feller," Kent concluded, "if I'd kept my big mouth shut you might not be in this fix."

"You know where these men are now?"

"I know where they were heading, so it shouldn't be too hard to follow their trail. The question is, how long will it be before you're fit to ride?"

Kent obviously assumed that Will would be out for vengeance once he was recovered. The man was being shrewd now where he had been guilty of careless talk before. He was also straight, otherwise he would not have come and confessed his responsibilities.

"You wouldn't be plannin' to ride with me, would you, Mr Kent?"

The smile returned. "The notion did cross my mind."

Weakened by multiple wounds in his chest, thigh, hip and left arm, Will sighed with helplessness. Here was a man ready and willing to help him exact justice for the attack against him, and yet Will knew it would be weeks before he was fit to ride again.

"You'll have a long wait, Mr Kent," he said dejectedly.

"While you take your time getting those wounds healed, I figured I might keep tabs on those bushwhackers. How does that idea grab you?"

Will eyed him speculatively as his depression lifted with remarkable speed. "I'd be much obliged."

"Anything else I can do for you?"

"Pour me some o' that barley water, will you? I've gotten a ragin' thirst."

9

KEITH JACKSON sat in a basket chair on the verandah and watched the two riders dismount. Father and daughter, he surmised, as he surveyed them. They fitted the descriptions Will Foreman had given of his employer and Clay's daughter. The man removed his hat to reveal an abundance of greying hair as he mopped his brow, and the girl was pretty and slender.

Clay flashed his teeth. "Howdy."

"Howdy, yourself. You wouldn't happen to be a rancher by the name of Clay, would you?"

The man gave a short laugh. "You psychic or something?"

"Will Foreman has been trained to describe people well. I guess you got his letter."

David Clay frowned in puzzlement.

"Letter? No, I received no letter. We came looking for a Mr Jackson to . . . "

"I'm Keith Jackson. I wrote that letter for Will. He was hurt too bad to do it himself. Pity you didn't get it before you left home. Never mind, you're here now, and that's more important."

Clay said, "Hurt? How?"

"Ambushed. He was shot up real bad."

The girl gave a gasp of fear.

"How is he? Will he . . . ?" Her father hesitated, his voice echoing Henrietta's concern.

"He'll live. He's a tough boy."

"Where can we find him?"

"Inside. If you wouldn't mind giving me a hand out of this chair, I'll take you to him."

As he helped Jackson out of his chair, Clay explained, "We came to see you hoping you would have news of Will. We couldn't understand why he hadn't come back to the ranch. We knew his plan was to visit you and then come back."

"I guessed that."

A minute and a half later they were standing beside Will Foreman's bed, the visitors alarmed by the sight of the still form with closed eyes.

"Looks like he dozed off."

Jackson's voice, as he had known it would, roused Will.

Clay put on a smile. "Hello, Will."

Still drowsy, Will acknowledged his visitors. "Mr Clay. Miss Henrietta."

"Hello, Will," the girl said softly.

His surprise at their visit was plain to see. "You got my letter then," he assumed.

"No, Will," Clay said sombrely. "We knew something must've happened to you, so we came looking."

Jackson indicated a couple of wooden chairs. "Take the weight off your feet. I'll leave you folks to talk."

He shuffled away. Will watched him go and prayed he would not be reduced to such limitations by his own wounds. He turned his attention back to his visitors as they pulled up chairs alongside his bed, sitting close together. The look of sadness in Henrietta's eyes warmed him, but he was puzzled by the fact that her mother had allowed her to visit him.

"This seems like a good place to be if you're sick," Clay said, looking around.

"Yeah. Sorry, boss. Don't reckon I'll be any use to you for quite a spell." He laughed gently, "I'm on the mend, but they tell me I was shot up pretty bad."

"I can wait, Will. The job will still be there when you're ready."

"Thanks." He shifted his glance to Henrietta. "Did you enjoy the ride, Miss Clay?"

"My name is Henrietta, Will. And yes, I did enjoy the ride, but I would have enjoyed it more if we hadn't been so worried about you." She glanced at her father. "Daddy has been quite concerned."

"My wife thought you'd run out on us, Will. I knew she was wrong."

That was the trouble with these

middle-aged women, Will told himself, they were always so damned sure they were right about everything.

"Thanks, boss," he said appreciatively.

"I knew you would have come back if you could," Henrietta chirped in support.

She had a very pleasant voice, Will recognized. Kind of musical. He wondered if she could sing.

A long, uncomfortable silence followed, none of them knowing the right thing to say and afraid of making a gaffe.

They stayed for almost an hour, then Clay decided their presence was tiring the wounded man. "We'll stay the night in town, Will, then come back and see you tomorrow, if you feel up to receiving visitors."

"I'd like that. Thanks for trustin' me an' bein' concerned."

"Is there anything you need?" Henrietta asked.

Just to see your smiling face, Will thought, but decided not to risk offending her father by putting the wish into words. "Not a thing," he said, summoning a smile.

* * *

It was another two weeks before he was allowed to sit in a chair beside his bed, and a further week before he was permitted to walk. His legs were surprisingly weak but the wound in his thigh was healing well. He spent a lot of time sitting and chatting with Keith Jackson and got to know Alastair Fox, who was there because of lung trouble. The mountain air was supposed to effect a recovery, but the man was alarmingly pale still, even after two months in the retreat.

Nigel Kent came twice to report that he had kept tabs on Ian Gilman and Gareth Keegan, the two men who had sided Anthony Newcombe in the shoot-out.

"I met up with them again in Castle Rock. This time I was careful not to mention your name."

"Good for you."

Impatient for recovery, Will accepted that he was lucky to be alive, yet nevertheless he was irritated by the restrictions his wounds had placed upon him. He was also worried by the fact that Keith Jackson seemed to be making no progress in his own recuperation. Jackson had never been a man with a ready smile, but now his eyes had lost that steely glint Will had always known. Robbed of his life's work, Jackson seemed to be slowly retreating into a cocoon of his own making. Moving around pained him and it was only when the other convalescents came to sit beside him that he was able to indulge in conversation. That did not seem to bother him and, with no known relatives he was, Will recognized, left with nothing but his memories.

"Dammit! Don't you die on me, Jackson!" Will muttered to himself in one of his own dejected moments.

★ ★ ★

"What's holdin' me up, Doc?" Will asked Doctor Wayne Yardley during an examination of his wounds.

"Holding you up!" the doctor exclaimed in astonishment. "Nothing is holding you up, Mr Foreman. You have made remarkably good progress. Most men would have died from so many gunshot wounds. This one in your chest missed your lung by no more than an inch and the bullet in your hip could have crippled you for life. You lost an enormous amount of blood and that made you very weak. You can *walk*, so be thankful. Your thigh is now completely healed and the shoulder wound is doing very nicely. Holding you up, indeed! You should get down on your knees and thank God for His healing hand on you. Patience, Mr Foreman, patience!"

Thoroughly chastened, Will lapsed into silence. The doc was right, as Keith Jackson confirmed when Will related the conversation to him later.

"Didn't I always tell you that patience is a virtue, Will? You've learned all I taught you pretty good, but patience I can't give you. That's something you have to learn for yourself, otherwise it'll be the death of you."

So you keep telling me, Will said to himself irritably, yet knowing the old man was right. He had done his best to quell his natural impetuosity but he seemed to have made little progress. More than once it had only been Jackson's restraining hand that had stopped him rushing in where wiser men would not have ventured. Only with horses had he ever been able to exercise patience.

"Telegraph for you from Chicago, Mr Jackson," the nurse announced as she handed it to the old man.

Jackson read it and put it into one of his pockets, making no comment. Will was itching to know what the message was but he dared not inquire.

If Jackson wanted him to know, then he would tell him.

Now what the hell is he up to? Will asked himself in frustration.

Keith Jackson knew exactly what his former lieutenant was thinking. He also knew it would do nothing for Will's peace of mind if he was made aware of what the telegraph had contained.

10

WITH the weeks stretching into months, the healing process in Will Foreman accelerated. He followed Doctor Yardley's advice and noticed he was getting stronger each day.

"Start with short walks, going a little farther each day, then when your legs feel strong, take short rides to get your body accustomed to sitting in a saddle again. You'll find riding will sap your energy very quickly at first, so don't try to be too ambitious."

The flexibility in his wrists and fingers was not as easy as before and so he practised handling his gun for half an hour each day, then progressed to some shooting. At first he was way off target, but gradually, as his hands became supple again, so his aim improved.

"I suppose you'll go hunting those bushwhackers as soon as you can ride again?" Jackson said.

"Wouldn't you?"

The belligerence in Will's voice did not upset the old man, who, although the fire had gone out of his belly, knew it was a natural thing for Will to want to do.

"Don't rush into anything until you're back to your best, otherwise you could be plucking harp strings before your time."

Will knew Jackson was right, as usual, and so he restrained his impatience to leave the convalescent home, in spite of being egged on by Nigel Kent, who became increasingly eager to set right the wrong he had done, but not without Will Foreman's help. Or at least that was his explanation. Will believed him. What worried him was the knowledge that Keith Jackson disliked the man, although he had confided no reason. It niggled in his mind like a rash that called for frequent scratching.

Three days before Will planned to go off with Nigel Kent to hunt down Gareth Keegan and Ian Gilman, Keith Jackson had a visitor.

"I've just finished an assignment in New Mexico," Henry Dupré explained. "Heard about your trouble. Thought I'd drop by and see how you were doing."

"This is a good place to be. They're looking after me well."

Will was sitting with Jackson at the time of Dupré's arrival. They had met only once before, when Will had been detailed to break Dupré out of the jail in Woodville, Arizona, to save the Pinkerton man from a hanging, although Will knew more about the little man by reputation. Deadly with a knife and no mean hand with a gun.

"What happened to you, Will?"

"Somebody had the idea o' turnin' me into a colander. It came as a surprise. If they'd notified me o' their intention . . ."

Dupré smiled. "Ambushed, huh?"

"Somethin' like that."

"Where are you headed, Henry?" Jackson queried.

"Denver."

Will knew better than to ask about his assignment. He left the two men to talk. Nigel Kent was hovering, his visit with Alastair Fox at an end, eager to discuss plans with Will.

* * *

Keegan and Gilman were on the run, after robbing a small bank in a town of no more than five hundred inhabitants. They had eluded the posse and headed into the mountains. The sheriff and his deputies had given up the chase, but Kent told Will he knew how to locate the outlaws' hide-out.

"How come you're so well informed? Why didn't you lead the posse to them?"

"Didn't hear about it soon enough. As to knowing the whereabouts of their hide-out, they think I'm on the wrong side of the law, too, so they don't see me as a threat."

"What did you tell 'em to give that impression?"

"They asked me one time what I did for a living, besides being lucky with the cards. I said I used my wits, hoping to gain their confidence. It worked. I got an invitation to step into Newcombe's boots, though I don't figure they planned to let me take over as leader."

The explanation did not entirely satisfy Will. "How *do* you make your livin', Nigel?"

Kent threw him a grin. "When my luck in the saloons runs out, I do anything that's on offer."

"Like what?"

"Roping and branding in the round-ups; riding shotgun on the stage; anything that's going at the time."

"So you'd call yourself a professional gambler?"

Kent's ham-like hands were nothing

like those of the card-sharps Will had known.

"That I am. I make out pretty good."

His suspicions mollified by the knowledge that there was an increasing number of men disillusioned by the poor rewards for riding herd on ranches and fixing fences, Will decided he could not afford to be choosy about his allies when Nigel Kent was all that was on offer. Kent seemed genuinely contrite about being responsible for Anthony Newcombe and his pards lying in wait for Will more than five months ago. Once they had caught up with Keegan and Gilman he could part company with Kent and head back to the Clay ranch. Right now he knew that his body was not yet ready to be tossed around by wild, bucking broncs, but given time, he could get back to the comparative peace of wrangling as opposed to the guns of outlaws.

They camped that night in the lower

reaches, with clear water running close by, and the hope that frost would not be severe. Nigel Kent was no mean hand with the skillet and he seemed to have accepted that he would do the cooking.

After they had eaten he wanted to talk. Will had already tabbed him as the garrulous type.

"That Jackson feller . . . he seems a mite old to be chasing after outlaws," he said for openers.

"You cain't judge Keith Jackson by other men. He's a one-off. There'll never be another like him."

"How do you mean?"

"He's gotten the art of survival down to a fine point. He's as good with a gun as any man I ever met."

Kent's head tilted sideways as he digested Will's words. "You mean he's one of these fast-draw fellers?"

"No, I don't mean that at all. But he don't waste lead. When he fires at a man he hits the target. His aim is jest about perfect."

Pride glinted in Will's brown eyes as he talked about the man he had come to admire so much.

"An' he's canny. He never goes into battle against outlaws without a plan."

"Then how come he got shot up so bad?"

"I guess he came up against a man as cunnin' as they come, but remember that Jackson lived. The other feller didn't."

"You talk like you love that old man."

Will remembered a girl saying the same thing to him one time and it brought back sad memories of what might have been. He chose not to respond to Kent's assumption.

"You two were together for seven years, you said."

"An' a bit. He taught me all I know. I'd've been dead long ago if it hadn't been for Mr Jackson."

They drank the last of the coffee in silence. Will knew Kent was eyeing him speculatively, wanting to talk still, while Will himself succumbed to his memories. There had been times of success and joy with Jackson, times of life-threatening danger, plus inevitable disappointments. Finding Jackson gut-shot in that canyon was one of the worst of them, vying for prominence in his mind with the time a girl in Woodville, Arizona, had stopped a bullet intended for him. That was a tragic moment that would haunt him all his days, and now he knew that Keith Jackson would not live much longer. The hardships wrought on his body by long rides, deprivation and gun battles with lawbreakers had taken their toll, and with no kin to bother about him, he no longer had anything to look forward to in old age. Sadness wrapped itself around Will, until Nigel Kent broke into his thoughts again.

"Will you go back to wrangling, Will?"

Will sighed heavily. "I guess so. I allus wanted a quiet life, but I couldn't leave Mr Jackson afore he decided to quit."

"But now you're free."

"I guess."

"But will your body stand up to all that rough riding after what you've been through these last months?"

"Only time will tell."

There was a short lull in the conversation before Kent asked, "Tell me about some of the outlaws you and Jackson tangled with."

Will stood up and stretched himself, feeling the effects of the long ride, but he was not yet sleepy, so he began telling Kent about some of the proudest moments he had experienced alongside Keith Jackson. Every now and then Kent would interject a comment or put a question, but eventually Will decided he'd talked enough.

"Well, I think I'll turn in."

Kent made no comment, his eyes lowered, deep in thought. He was still sitting hunched by the fire when Will rolled himself into his soogans and closed his eyes. Had he known what Nigel Kent was thinking he would not have fallen asleep so easily.

Kent now had all the information he needed.

11

"YOU ever actually been to this hide-out, Nigel?"

They were saddling up after breakfast, getting ready to continue the pursuit of Ian Gilman and Gareth Keegan.

"I've never actually been there, but from the directions they gave me, I figure it won't be hard to find."

"What makes you think they'll be there?"

"It's no more than a hunch, but where else would they go?"

"I dunno, but my experience is that when outlaws know the heat is on, — they cross the State line, thinking that's the safest thing t'do."

Another question reared its ugly head in Will's mind. "Why did they give you those instructions?"

"In case I changed my mind about

stepping into Newcombe's boots. Seems they'd always found this place safe from posse pursuit in the past, so I figured that's where they'd go. We'd gotten real friendly and I think they felt a bit lost without their leader. I figure they just had to make that last bank raid to prove to themselves they could get along without Newcombe."

It sounded plausible, but Will was beginning to have some doubts about Nigel Kent's altruism. For a man who loved life in a saloon he seemed to be putting himself out some to rectify his mistake in talking about Keith Jackson and Will Foreman to the outlaws. How could he be sure it had been *his* big mouth that had helped to set up Will for the kill?

He chided himself for being uncharitable. Not many men would have gone and confessed responsibility to the victim of three gunmen.

He forked the roan and watched Nigel Kent kick dirt over the dying embers of the fire. That done, they headed farther into the mountains, intent on making the best of an early start. Kent took the lead, making himself responsible for spotting the landmarks he had been told to use as a guide to the outlaws' hide-out.

"If these two varmints have proved to themselves they can get along without Newcombe, mebbe they won't want you to join 'em," Will pushed into a long silence.

Kent grinned back at him. "They like a third man. Makes bank robbing easier. Besides, that ain't why we're headed after them, is it?"

"No, but when they see you they'll think you've come to team up with them."

"They'll know different when they see you."

"Yeah."

Another long silence fell between them.

They passed the mouth of the canyon where Keith Jackson had killed Randolph Carter, and Will relived his abortive climb to the peaks in his effort to get the drop on Eddie Arnold. A kind of fury built up inside him as he reflected on his failure and the bullet that had crippled Jackson. He resolved not to make the same mistake in his quest to wreak vengeance on Gilman and Keegan.

Towards noon the going became more hazardous. Kent had come upon the cone of rock standing up in isolation, pointing the way to a narrow, little-used trail, taking them higher up the mountain. It seemed to Will an odd place for outlaws to choose in getting away from pursuit by a posse and yet, when he thought more about it, men hunting fugitives would hardly be likely to give a second thought to it.

They came to an old trapper's cabin, still standing firmly but long since fallen into disuse, full of debris blown by the harsh winds that whipped through the Rocky Mountains in winter. The rotting corpse of a bear that had taken refuge from the snows during the last winter and failed to survive gave off a pungent smell, making both men wrinkle their noses.

"Must've been an old 'un comin' to the end of his days," Will surmised.

"I'm sure glad _I_ didn't get caught up here last winter," Kent commented forcefully.

Will echoed the sentiment. Raised in the heat of Texas, he had never gotten used to harsh cold weather.

"You sure we're on the right track, Nigel?"

"I think so, though it is getting hard to follow. I'm sure that must be the cabin they mentioned."

An hour later they smelled burning timber and allowed their noses to lead them.

"You think it could be them?" Will asked, drawing alongside his new partner.

"Doubt it. I figure the hide-out is a few miles away from here. Let's take a look."

Below the track was a small lake and,

as they made their way slowly down the slope, smoke spiralled upwards. Somebody had put fresh timber on to a fire.

They hitched their horses to a couple of pines and moved lower down on foot. A man was making fresh coffee over the fire. He seemed to be alone, although two horses grazed by the lake some distance away. The man looked up as they came within rock-throwing distance. He offered a welcoming smile. Reassured, Will and Nigel Kent went to meet him.

"Howdy! You're just in time. Java's about ready. You got mugs?"

"Back with the horses," Kent said, nodding in the direction from which they had come.

"Go get 'em."

"I'll go, Will," Kent offered.

"Where you fellers headed?"

He was a young man with a ready smile, brown friendly eyes and hair on the lighter shade of brown.

"Farther up the mountain," Will

answered. "Didn't expect to meet anybody around here."

"I'm headed south," he gave out with a self-conscious laugh. "Ran into more trouble than I could handle back in Denver."

"Some tough hombres in that town," Will said laconically, wondering what kind of trouble the man meant. He didn't look much like a lawbreaker but you could never tell by appearances.

Will turned to see Kent coming back with their mugs, then gave his attention back to the man offering them hospitality. Just as he was looking forward to a hot drink he felt a heavy blow at the back of his head, and bright sunlight swiftly changed to complete blackness.

"Nice work, Kent," the young man said.

Kent dropped the heavy piece of timber he had picked up after he'd gotten the tin mugs from saddlebags. Will Foreman had failed to notice the right hand held behind Kent's back, his concentration relaxed by the *bonhomie* of the young man's welcome.

"Worked out better than we thought. Where's Gilman?"

"Right here," a voice called in answer.

"Ian Gilman strode along from the direction in which the horses had been picketed on long ropes. He looked down at Will Foreman from under black, bushy brows. "I'll never know how he managed to live after all the lead we threw at him five months ago, but he'll not survive again."

"We still gonna do it the way you said, Gil?" Keegan asked, his smile full of anticipatory glee.

"Yeah. It'll be nice and slow. Pity we can't hang around and watch, but I hate to see a man suffering."

From beneath that huge moustache, Nigel Kent asked a question. "What have you boys got in mind?"

"You'll see," Gilman replied grimly.

★ ★ ★

He knew before he opened his eyes that he was stark naked. The fresh wind on his skin had a kind of soothing effect, but his head ached abominably. He wished he had never awakened from his slumbers. Funny, but he could not move his legs, and his hands seemed to be tied wide on either side of him. He opened his eyes and saw that his left wrist was firmly roped to a stake in the ground. Turning his head the other way, he found another stake immobilizing his right hand.

"Has he come round yet?" a strange voice asked.

Will recognized Nigel Kent's answering deep baritone growl, "Yeah." Kent laughed harshly as Will looked up at him. "You sure look funny, Foreman, staked out there without your glad rags."

Will's arms were at full stretch, making it impossible for him to lift his shoulders, but as he tilted his head forward he could see his feet had been fastened to stakes too. Kent's eyes were on a point where Will's thighs began, almost level with his hip joints. He would have liked to think Kent's amusement was caused by Will's scars, but he knew it was not so.

The young man with the welcoming smile came into Will's range of vision. "You think we should cut it off?" he asked with relish.

"Oh, no," the third voice replied. "That'd be too quick. The wolves or the mountain lions will do that."

He looked Will straight in the eyes, a black-haired man with an equally black, bedraggled moustache that needed trimming, and continued, "They'll tear it off him." He shuddered at what he was thinking. "Ugh! Messy."

"Who the hell are you?" Will growled.

"The name's Gilman. My pard here is Keegan. We were siding Tony Newcombe when you killed him. We left you for dead, but this time we won't be using bullets." He moved closer and bent his knees until his buttocks were touching the heels of his boots. "The wolves and the pumas come down here to drink at night, and they'll find food ready an' waitin' for them. *You!*"

"You're mad."

"Ain't I just. Maybe you'll freeze to death before they get here . . . if you're lucky."

Will Foreman had experienced fear before, but nothing like this. Helpless, staked out under the hot sun worse than a plucked turkey, he contemplated what this sadistic man was saying, raw terror shafting through every nerve in his body.

Gilman went on. "Keegan pulled off your boots and pants before he tied your feet to the stakes, only he got kinda impatient when he came to your longjohns. Used his knife to rip 'em up. Scratched your flesh a mite. Those carnivores will smell blood and come a-running." He stood up and walked away. "Let's get going, boys."

"*Kent!*" Will screamed.

"I'm right here, Will."

The huge man stood in the V formed by Will's outstretched feet, a hard look in his eyes. Will didn't know why, but Kent had led him into a trap.

"Why?"

"Gil and Gareth told me you were the one who killed Allen Edwards in Woodville a couple of years back. I wasn't too sure they'd gotten it right, but you confirmed it with your own lips last night. Me and Allen, we grew up together. When I was a kid he was my best buddy. He saved me from drowning before I learned to swim. I owed him. I guess this settles the account."

"So it was all a big bluff."

"You could say that. I'm surprised you fell for it, you having been a Pinkerton man. I figured them fellers was smart, but we all make mistakes, I guess. Reckon this was your biggest."

"You coming with us, Nige?" Gilman called out, heading for his horse.

"Sure. So-long, sucker!"

Will heard the retreating footfalls and

cursed himself for a fool until all his emotional energy had been dissipated. Those men had known how to tie knots so that he could never get free. His only chance would be to pull the stakes out of the ground, and yet he knew before he began that any such attempt would be a fruitless exercise. Nevertheless he began straining with all the strength he could muster. Being torn apart while he was still alive by carnivorous marauders who would be quick to recognize his helplessness was a thought too horrifying to contemplate. The prospect drove him to frenzied efforts, until he was completely exhausted, his wrists and ankles rubbed raw by the chafing ropes.

After a while he began to pray, but it seemed that even God had gone deaf.

As the sun dipped behind the mountain peaks and the wind grew more chilly he closed his eyes and tried to numb his mind. Above him he caught the soft sounds of movement.

The killers were coming.

12

THEY must be ravenous, he decided. They were coming for him in a rush, eager to tear at his flesh, to taste the blood, to kill him by slow torture. The rushing noise in his ears was deafening.

Something was sawing at the rope binding his right wrist. He feared to open his eyes, but then realized it was a strange thing to happen when his fleshy parts were more easily accessible. Light dawned in the darkness. He opened his eyes as his wrist was freed.

Henry Dupré threw him a grin. "I ain't never seen a sight like this before."

It took him no more than a minute to cut through the bonds that had held Will Foreman fast for what had seemed like hours. His mind numbed by the fear of being ripped to pieces, it took all of that minute for Will to accept that prayers do get answered sometimes. He was puzzled by the sudden appearance of Dupré, but explanations could come later. Right now there was a large halo glistening over Henry Dupré's head.

The smoke-grey eyes shining out of a lean face had the light of joy in them. Small of frame, Dupré moved around very quickly and smoothly. "Reckon those longjohns are not much good to you any more, but if I were you I'd try and hang on to them for now. The rest of your clothes are over there."

Dupré nodded towards Will's left.

Will knew he had been lying on his ripped underwear, but now he found it difficult to cloak it around his body. At least those sadists had not cut off the buttons. There was a spare pair in his saddlebags, but he decided he would like a hot bath before he put them on.

"You've been bleeding some," Dupré reminded him. "You'd best go and wash that red off before you get dressed."

Gingerly Will walked down to the water, wanting to get rid of the smell of dried blood on his skin, yet concerned that he might start up the bleeding again. The water was ice-cold. He shuddered at its contact, then went back and tried again to wrap his ripped longjohns around him before pulling on his pants and shirt. His ankles had swelled and pulling on his boots was an uncomfortable task.

"My horse still up there?" he asked Dupré.

"Yes. Maybe they thought about taking it, but if they're headed back to that town below the nursing home it would raise a few questions. I guess they figured they'd really put an end to you this time. You could have frozen to death before morning, staked out as you were."

"I guess I owe you, Henry."

"You owe me nothing. Every time I think about you I feel a hemp rope around my neck. I'm just glad to have been given the chance to even things up."

"The water in that lake don't taste so good. Can we spare the time to heat coffee?"

Dupré looked up at the ever darkening sky before replying. "Your friends won't be coming back this way, so I guess we can make camp here as well as any other place. At least we're not short of kindling. Let's get started."

Later, their bodies fed and throats adequately oiled, Dupré said, "Kinda lucky for you I happened to be passing this way."

"Like hell!" Will retorted explosively. "You were trailin' me! That Jackson put you up to it, didn't he?"

"Sort of."

"An' that day you came to the nursing home . . . you weren't jest stoppin' by. You were sent!"

Dupré grinned slyly. "Mr Pinkerton did ask me to look in on you both. He's kinda thoughtful that way."

Will thought back to the telegraph Jackson had received and pushed into his pocket without a word of explanation.

"Well . . . tell me the rest, Henry."

There was a long pause while Dupré wondered where to begin. He knew Will would not be satisfied until he knew the full facts.

"Jackson was concerned about you, Will. Sort of wanted to save you from yourself."

"I guessed he was suspicious about Nigel Kent, an' I know he didn't like the man."

"Now you know why."

"No, I don't. Tell me."

Dupré pulled a cheroot from his pocket. He rasped a match on his Levis and put flame to tobacco, drew on it and examined the glow at its tip when he took it from between his lips, just the way Will had seen Keith Jackson do so often. Will contained his impatience with difficulty.

"You know Jackson," Dupré began.

"He's gotten a lot stored up in that head of his. He had a hunch about Kent. Sent a wire to Chicago asking for a rundown on him. When they looked into Allen Edward's background, up came the name of Nigel Kent. The rest you can guess."

"Yeah. Jackson decided I needed a minder. You got the job. I'm real grateful, Henry."

"Don't thank me, thank him."

Will was irritated with himself. After all those years with Jackson teaching him about survival he had been suckered yet again, and so easily, even after promising himself that he would not allow Keegan and Gilman to get the better of him a second time. And then Nigel Kent had rubbed salt into the wound with his disparaging remarks about men who worked for the Pinkerton Detective Agency. Mr Allan Pinkerton would not be pleased with Will Foreman if he ever heard about this latest episode.

"I should've known that Kent was too

plausible," Will conceded grudgingly.

Sensing Will's anger with himself, Henry Dupré tried to cheer him. "We all make mistakes."

"That's what *he* said."

Dupré was a naturally optimistic sort and his sunny disposition would not allow the lengthening silence between them to continue.

"What now, Will?"

"I've gotta get those bastards or I'll never be able to live with myself."

"They've gotten nearly half a day's start on us."

"Yeah, but if there's one thing I learned from Mr Jackson it's how to follow sign. I'll find 'em."

"*We'll* find them, Will," Dupré corrected firmly.

"You in on this?"

"I am. The rewards for Keegan and Gilman are not big, but I can always use an extra dollar. I've gotten leave from the Agency to do a little bounty hunting."

Will snapped his head sharply to look

back at the little executioner, for that was how Will always thought of him. "*Bounty hunting!*"

"That's what they call it, Will, when you hunt men for money."

"Money's got nothin' t'do with it as far as I'm concerned!"

Dupré fashioned a teasing grin. "You mean I can have your share?"

Will was on the point of exploding angrily when he remembered he owed his life to this little man. Then another thought struck him with some force.

"How come it took you so long to release me, anyway?"

"I had to hang back. Nearly lost you and Kent a couple of times, but I couldn't afford to get too close in case either of you spotted me." He gave a shrug. "After all, even that Jackson could've been wrong about Kent's motives."

"Jackson is *never* wrong," came the reluctant concession.

Dupré continued his explanation. "It was just lucky I spotted your horse hitched half-way down that slope there. I was puzzled. What had happened? I asked myself. Where was Kent's horse? I had to move around to try and find out what had been going on. It took me quite a spell. Even after I saw you staked out I couldn't be sure they weren't still around. I had to make certain."

It was a reasonable explanation and Will acknowledged that there was no way he could have been spared his struggles to get free, as well as the fear of being eaten alive by the mountain creatures.

Dupré tossed away the stub of his cheroot. "You will have to learn to be more choosy about your friends now you've ended your partnership with Jackson. Seems to me you've been right lucky to have spent all those years alongside him. I envy you."

Will could see that Dupré was serious. He wanted to ask his rescuer how he had learned to be so deadly with both knife and gun, prowess for which he was well known. Will wondered if the ruthless streak in the man had been inherited from a hard father or if it was something in his early life that had fashioned his attitude towards the ungodly.

"We ought to plan our strategy, Will, before we bed down."

When they had finished talking, Will settled down to sleep, his mind easier, his confidence in the outcome of his quest strengthened by the knowledge that he had a partner as cunning as Keith Jackson to help him. The trio who had left him as a tasty meal for wild animals would get their come-uppance.

13

GUNFIRE echoed across the canyon. Will Foreman drew rein and halted the roan to assess distance and angle as he looked down from the ridge. Who was doing the shooting? And why? Satisfied, he urged his mount forward, confident that Henry Dupré, following at a discreet distance according to plan, would also have been alerted.

Less than ten minutes later Will had a clear view of Nigel Kent, Ian Gilman and Gareth Keegan indulging in some harmless shooting practice. A haze of gunsmoke wafted higher in the canyon, carried away by the soft wind. Will could hardly believe his luck, catching up with them so soon, but then the outlaws would have no reason to hurry to their next destination, wherever that might be.

He decided to wait for Dupré to catch up with him. To go down there alone would be inviting more trouble than he could reasonably expect to handle.

"I've seen them," Dupré informed him as he drew alongside. "The plan still stands. We attack in a pincer movement. They'll be so surprised to see you again they won't give a thought to me. You go first and concentrate on Keegan and Kent. I'll take out Gilman."

The outlaws were reloading their guns when Will Foreman sent a rifle-bullet screaming across the canyon. All three men turned in the direction of the shot sound as it echoed in the mountain.

"Drop your guns an' get your hands in the air!" Will yelled at the top of his voice.

None of them seemed inclined to do that as they looked at each other. It was clear to Will that Kent recognized his voice. Gilman seemed to be suggesting it was not possible. An argument began amongst the three men.

Will moved closer, a fresh bullet in the breech. They all looked towards him again, now able to see him clearly, rifle held steadily and pointing their way. Will continued his forward movement.

Gilman turned on his pard, Keegan. "I thought you'd tied him up good, Gareth!"

"I did! There's no way he could have gotten loose!"

"Well he did, dammit! Or do you think that's a ghost you're looking at?"

The sneer in his voice withered Keegan.

"Drop the guns an' cut the cackle!" Will called, now no more than thirty yards away.

They each hesitated as they looked around. Seeing no one else, they were confident they could take him, even if he took one of them first. Nigel Kent appeared less sure of himself, afraid of being the victim, Will surmised. He played his hunch.

"Drop the gun, Kent!"

Fury suddenly overcame the big man's apprehension and he lifted his gun. Will shot him before he could fire. Keegan threw himself to the ground, firing as he fell. The shot missed Will by a large margin. Will dropped to his knees and fired again, catching Keegan in the shoulder and sending him rolling away in agony.

Meantime Dupré had emerged from cover and taken a hand and Gilman was lying quite still. Both Will and Dupré ran towards the outlaws.

Will picked up Keegan's fallen Colt pistol and hurled it away with a mighty swing of his right arm. Dupré knew he had killed Gilman but he nevertheless turned him over to make doubly sure. The vacant eyes turned skywards, no longer able to see anything.

Nigel Kent was softly moaning. Will's rifle shot had hit him in the chest but apparently missed both heart and lungs. The big man was writhing in agony.

Away to his right, Gareth Keegan was clutching his left shoulder, his face contorted with pain, his right hand awash with blood.

Henry Dupré's face registered annoyance. "I never did like taking prisoners. They're a damned nuisance."

"Mebbe they'll bleed to death afore we get 'em back to civilization," Will responded cheerfully.

Kent stared up at Will with hate-filled eyes, but fright tempered his fury. He was fearful that Will Foreman and this little man would stake *him* out and leave him to die.

"It wasn't my idea, Will," he said pleading. "It was Gilman. I had to go along with what him and Keegan had planned. I didn't . . . "

"You didn't think I'd ever get free!" Will interposed angrily. "You *liked* the idea o' wolves tearin' me apart while I was still breathin'. You tricked me, Kent, had me think you were a friend, an' now you're gonna pay."

"No, Will, no! You wouldn't, you

couldn't." A sickly smile formed beneath the huge moustache. "You're not like that."

"He ain't, but I am," Dupré said softly, menace dripping from his lips.

Will shot a sharp glance at Dupré, wondering if he meant it or if he was just trying to scare the living daylights out of the big man. He piled on the agony. "You want me to gather some stakes, Henry?"

"You do that, Will, while I get his boots off."

Gareth Keegan sat up, holding his shoulder, accepting the pain and the bleeding stoically. The bigger man, physically stronger, had failed to show the same resolution. The icy coldness in Henry Dupré's voice, advancing with the intention of giving Nigel Kent a taste of what Will Foreman had been forced to endure, drove the big man into frenzied panic. Before Dupré could touch him, Kent scrambled to his feet and ran towards his horse, but the effort demanded too much on both heart and lungs, pumping the blood from his chest at a rapidly increasing rate. As he reached out to grab the reins he fell forward, stumbled to his knees, and then rolled over on to his back, his strength ebbing away fast. The two men ambled after him, halted, and saw the blood oozing out of him.

"He'll be dead in an hour," Dupré told Will, without a trace of emotion.

Will began to understand how Dupré had survived so many dangerous encounters; the man was gifted with a brain so cold and calculating that he was never swayed by sympathy for those he deemed did not deserve it.

They drank the Java the outlaws had been brewing while they indulged in shooting practice. Will gave some to Keegan, who looked up at him with cold, hate-filled eyes. Subdued by pain and the loss of his gun, Keegan picked up the tin mug Will set down beside him and slowly drank the hot liquid, feeling its warmth giving him renewed strength. The leaden slug that had been driven into him at an angle was still in his shoulder and he knew that if he did not die from the bleeding, then lead poisoning would hasten his journey into hell if Will Foreman and his pard did not get him to a doctor. When he fastened his gaze onto Henry Dupré he realized how his good work in tying up Foreman had been negated. Like Gilman and Kent, he had fully expected the mountain creatures to indulge in a feast presented to them so temptingly.

"You still want that reward money, Henry?" Will queried after a long silence.

"Why not? It would be a crime not to claim it."

"We takin' them all with us?"

Dupré considered the problem for only a brief time before giving Will his solution. "Just Keegan. He'll be only too keen to tell the law what happened to the other two, hoping to make it look bad for us."

"We gonna bury them? That's if

you're right about Kent dyin' within the hour."

"Did you happen to bring along a shovel?"

"No, I didn't."

"Then I guess they'll just have to be left to the buzzards, or whatever scavengers get here first."

It was not an idea that found favour with Will Foreman. "I'd rather we threw them over their horses and delivered them to the law office."

Dupré shrugged. "If it will make you feel better."

"It will. I've seen what buzzards can do to a corpse."

"You know, Will, there's a touch of the sentimental about you. I can see why you wanted to quit the Agency and go back to wrangling." He let out a deep sigh with a shake of the head. "Still, to each his own."

Dupré *was* right. When they went to look at Nigel Kent again he was no longer breathing, his pulse stilled in death.

14

"I'LL look after Keegan, you take care of the stiffs," Dupré said in a voice that expected no argument.

Will accepted that it was a fair arrangement. He was the one who had been reluctant to leave the dead men to the scavengers, while Dupré was intent on claiming the reward money for Gilman and Keegan.

"No reward out for Kent?" Will queried as they went to lift the dead men on to their own horses.

"As far as we know he never broke the law once. What he told you about himself was true, unless he's committed crimes without ever being connected with them."

"That don't add up, Henry. Why would he have turned so vicious if he was a law-abidin' citizen? If you'd seen the way he looked at me just before the three o' them left me staked out you'd know he was full of hate."

"Towards you, maybe, but not the world in general." They faced each other across the haunches of Kent's horse. "What happens between men in their childhood lasts a lifetime. He owed his life to a man you killed in Woodville."

"So he told me."

"Well then, there's your answer. Allen Edwards turned outlaw, Nigel Kent became a gambler, but when luck turned against him he didn't go in for robbing and killing. He went to work to get himself a fresh stake. Kent was basically an honest man. Not addicted to work, but willing when necessity demanded."

At least the man had told Will the truth about that. He felt a momentary sadness at the thought of how easily a man's mind can become warped.

Will put a rope through the bridles of the dead men's horses and attached it to his saddle-horn, while Dupré collected

Keegan's mount and led it towards the wounded outlaw, still sitting nursing his shoulder. Will followed him.

Keegan looked up at Dupré as the little man stood in front of him.

"Tell me something, Keegan . . . was Kent with you on that bank raid in Carlton?"

"No. It was just me and Gilman."

"Was he ever with you on robberies?"

Keegan forced a smile of immense satisfaction. "Tough luck, mister, but you ain't gonna claim any reward for Kent."

Dupré glanced at Will, his eyes asking if his partner was satisfied with what Keegan had told him. Will nodded, almost imperceptibly.

Dupré pulled Keegan's rifle from the saddle-boot, broke it open and extracted the shells, putting them into his own pocket. Then he replaced the rifle in the boot. A search of the saddle-bags revealed a box of pistol shells, but as the man had been deprived of his Colt pistol, he replaced the box. The loops in Keegan's gun-belt were half-empty, but Dupré took the precaution of removing those that remained and pocketed them.

"There, Keegan, now all your teeth have been drawn. Get yourself off your ass and into the saddle. We're moving."

Painfully, very slowly, Keegan pushed himself upright, paused to take deep breaths as he collected the reins with his left hand and put his right on the saddle-horn. His face was a mask of pain. He made no protest when Dupré gave him a leg-up into the saddle.

For a brief moment Will wondered why Dupré had not manacled his prisoner, but then he guessed the little gunfighter had no fear of Keegan attempting to escape. Pain and loss of blood had weakened him too much, and Will knew that Dupré would not hesitate to kill Keegan if he should be crazy enough to try to make a run for it. He figured Keegan would be in no ·

doubt about that, either.

Dupré walked across to his own horse, an Appaloosa, and forked the saddle.

"Head towards Carlton, Keegan. I'll be right behind you."

The party headed west, with Dupré riding alongside Will Foreman, the other two horses following in procession, carrying the victims of their own folly.

* * *

They rode into Carlton as the sun dipped low the following day, their prisoner badly in need of medical attention. The town marshal was lukewarm in his reception, but the mayor, who just happened to be in the law office at the time, beamed with pleasure.

"These the men who robbed the bank?"

Dupré confirmed it. He told the two officials all he knew about the wounded Keegan and the two dead men, then requested the reward money.

"We'll need witnesses to confirm these are the right men before we pay out," the marshal warned him.

"You doubting my word, Marshal?"

"No, I ain't, but then neither am I so dumb as to believe ever'thing I'm told by men I ain't never seen before. I need irrefutable evidence, mister."

Dupré moved over to Gareth Keegan, lying with closed eyes on the bench seat by the window.

"Keegan!"

The outlaw opened weary eyes and stared back at his captor.

"You want to see a doctor? That bullet troubling you?"

"Yeah."

"Well before you get any help, the marshal wants to know if it was you and Gilman who held up the bank here in Carlton."

"Yeah, yeah, it was. Will you get the doc, for pity's sake?"

Dupré turned back to the marshal. "That good enough for you?"

"Sure it is," the mayor answered for him. "I'll go get Doc Freeman. Best get him on a cell cot before he falls to the floor, Marshal Lichfield." He moved hastily to the door, then turned around. "Looks like we'll have to pay these men. They've earned the reward money."

* * *

The Carlton Hotel was surprisingly modern, Will Foreman decided, a ripple of pleasure running through him as he entered the room allocated to him and Henry Dupré. Comfort was something he had gotten accustomed to in the mountain nursing home and, as yet, he had not realized how much he preferred sleeping in a bed, rather than a bunk.

After supper the two men separated, Will to sit quietly in the hotel lounge, while Dupré went in search of fun. I guess he wants a woman, Will surmised. Wearied by almost four full days in the saddle and the ordeal of being staked out naked under the sun, Will felt no such desires. He was content to sit and contemplate his immediate future for a spell.

There was a job waiting for him with David Clay, but the past few days were a warning that his body was not yet ready for the challenge of breaking in wild horses. It was little more than a day's ride to Denver, and from there he could take the train to Ellsworth, where Keith Jackson's friend was probably still keeping her hotel running. She would be saddened to learn about what had happened to the man she had known since childhood, but Will felt she would want to know and the urge to inform her was strong. He thought of writing a letter and then heading back to see the old man, yet he knew that a personal visit from him would be more acceptable to Queenie Parsons.

The decision made, he got to his feet

and went in search of a hot bath.

When Dupré eventually came back to their room Will told him about his decision.

"Then we can ride together, once we've gotten that reward money. I was heading for Denver anyhow."

There was a contented smile on Dupré's lips as he got into bed and Will guessed he was well satisfied with his evening adventure.

They spent just one night in Denver, then, to Will's surprise, Henry Dupré decided he would take the train with him to Ellsworth.

"I don't need a nursemaid for this trip, Henry."

"I got nothing better to do for the next week or so. Besides, you do have a habit of getting into trouble, and I did promise the old man I'd watch out for you."

Will allowed himself a wry smile. He would be glad of Dupré's company.

★ ★ ★

"Now ain't that a shame," Dupré murmured as they stood gazing into the open space where 'Queenie's House' had stood.

"Must've been some fire!" Will commented with feeling. "Wonder what happened to Queenie?"

"That, Will, is something I'm itching to find out."

Will turned his head to hold Dupré's determined gaze. A feminine voice cut into their contemplations.

"Texas Will! Is it really you?"

The exclamation, followed by the questioning lilt, made Will turn and face the young woman staring at him. Only for a brief moment did he hesitate, then returned her beaming smile.

"Angela Fielding," he breathed in admiration. "An' more beautiful than ever."

"Careful, Will. I'm a married woman now."

"Aw, shucks!" he teased. "An' I figured you was gonna wait for me!"

She laughed musically, while Will

unashamedly admired the near-chestnut hair, beautifully coiffured, with not a strand out of place. The cleavage he remembered was tastefully covered by a lace-embroidered, high-necked dress.

"You look like you married the banker!"

"Flatterer! Aren't you going to introduce me to your friend?"

He turned to Dupré with a touch of embarrassment. "Oh, I'm sorry. Henry, this is Angela Fielding."

"I heard you mention her name," Dupré returned with a strong note of sarcasm.

"Angela, meet Henry Dupré."

She held out a gloved hand, expecting Dupré to shake it gently. Instead, he lifted her hand and touched her fingers with his lips. "You are the most enchanting creature I've seen in months," he said, gazing into eyes with strong hints of green in them.

She looked back at Will when Dupré released her hand. "Is he giving you lessons in charm, Will? I seem to recall you used to be the shy type."

"That was seven years ago, Angela. I've been around a bit since then."

"I gathered that much from what you said about me waiting for you." Then her tone changed. "What gall you have, to even suggest I'd wait seven years for you."

"Jest my sense o' humour. Figured you'd know that."

Her smile flashed again. "Of course I did."

"That husband of yours is a lucky cuss. Do I get to meet him?"

"Not on your life! Why, you're even more handsome than you were seven years ago. My husband would probably shoot you on sight, and maybe me, too."

Henry Dupré began to feel he was going to be shut out again. "Well if you two former sweethearts want to talk about old times, I'll mosey along and quench my thirst. S'long Mrs . . . ?"

"Norris. And Will was right, I *did* marry the banker."

"Well . . . like I said . . . "

"Hold it, Henry. Mebbe Angela can help us." He faced the woman again. "You fancy a cup o' coffee, Angela?"

She hesitated, looking from one to the other. "I really shouldn't be seen talking to strange men . . . "

"We're not strange men!" Will protested.

"Well . . . I suppose there's safety in numbers. Not as if I had an assignation with just *one* good-looking man."

"You are most kind," Dupré responded softly, "and we do need information. I guess you might be able to supply it, you being a resident here."

"Oh, all right. Let's go to Hestor Jibbert's place."

"She still here?" Will queried.

"Yes, Will, she's still here. Where would you expect her to be? She's lived here most of her life."

The café proprietress had collected a few grey hairs since Will Foreman had last seen her, but the coffee was still first-class. With cups in front of them, the earlier banter of the two men evaporated in their eagerness to find out about the burning down of 'Queenie's House'. Will asked Angela Norris about it.

"They said it was arson, but they couldn't prove it. No one is really sure."

"An' Queenie?"

"She's in the hospital. She was burned."

Dupré and Will looked earnestly at each other, then the little man asked, "How do we get to the hospital, Mrs Norris?"

15

RECOGNITION came a little slowly as Queenie Parsons looked into Will Foreman's smiling face.

"Hello, Mrs Parsons. Remember me? Will Foreman."

"The young man who came with Keith Jackson some years back."

"That's right."

"You've grown into quite a man."

Will flushed with embarrassment. "You remember Henry? He tells me he stayed with you several times."

She looked into the little man's eyes. "Oh, yes, I remember Henry. Still wowing the ladies with that oily charm of yours, are you, Henry?"

Dupré put on an expression of injured pride. "Queenie! There's nothing oily about my charm."

"That's what you think! Or is it?

Expect you know very well what a woman-cheating skunk you are right enough. What are you doing here?"

Will Foreman was a little alarmed at the exchange of words between the two of them, thinking perhaps it had been a mistake to let Dupré come along with him, but his mind was soon set at rest. In the next few minutes it became clear that, although Queenie might deplore Dupré's womanizing, she respected him for his other qualities.

"We just found out about the fire, Queenie."

"I see." She stared hard at Dupré. "Who sent you?"

"Nobody. We're not here on official business. Like I said, we only just found out about the fire."

"How?"

"We'd planned to stay with you a couple of nights. It didn't please us none to find that big empty space. Understand it only happened three weeks ago?"

"Yes." She looked away from him,

her eyes clouding with the memory of it. Then anger flashed at them both. "All the work I put into that place, ploughing back all the profits with extensions, and now there's nothing left. Somebody is going to pay when I get out of here."

"It was arson then?" Will asked her.

"It was, whatever anyone else might say."

The two men looked at each other, then back at Queenie, their eyes surveying the bandages on her left arm and around her scalp. They both suspected that her hair must have caught fire in the blaze and, if their suspicions were correct, she was no longer the beauty they had both known. The dressing on the left side of her face looked ominous. Although she called herself *Mrs* Parsons whenever her status came into conversation, they both knew she had never been married and only used the ring on her left hand to ward off men who might see her as a desirable catch.

"We heard you did a good rescue act with your guests." Henry pushed into the silence. "That how you got yourself burned?"

"No. I went back for the cash box. There wasn't much in it, but there wasn't much in the bank, either. I'd just paid for the latest extension."

The significance of that admission was apparent to both men. At the end of another hiatus, Dupré asked her straight out, "You broke, Queenie?"

"Almost, Henry."

Will looked away, his mind racing, unable to cope with the mixture of dejection and anger in the woman's eyes. Rage began to build inside him. If the fire truly had been started deliberately, then he knew Keith Jackson would want him to do something about it.

He did not raise his head as he asked, "D'you know who was responsible, Mrs Parsons?"

"Yes, Mr Foreman, I do."

Now he looked at her. "Mebbe me an' Henry could do somethin' about that."

"It's not your concern, young Will."

"Mr Jackson would want me to *make* it my concern."

"Keith?" She smiled for the first time. "How is the old buzzard? Those outlaws haven't got him yet?"

He played with his hat. "That's what we came to town to tell you, ma'am. He was hurt bad a while back. Didn't you read about it in the papers?"

"I never read newspapers. Full of gossip and inaccurate reporting."

"Well, we were chasin' two fugitives from a train robbery, an' Mr Jackson was gut-shot. It was touch an' go for a while, but he pulled through in the end. Only he ain't well, ma'am, he ain't well a-tall. Doctors don't give him more'n a year."

"I'm real sorry to hear that. He's a good man. I owe him a lot. Best friend I ever had."

"Me too."

"Have to be realistic, though. It had to happen some day. No man is immortal, and in your business . . . "

She left the prognosis unfinished.

"Yeah, I guess you're right."

Dupré butted in. "Not much we can do for old Keith, Queenie, but I reckon we could take a shot at rectifying *your* problem, so how about giving us a few details?"

"You just heard me tell young Will it wasn't his fight. No more is it yours."

"Now don't you go upsetting me, Queenie. I'm not the sort who takes kindly to being affronted, and like Will, I know what Jackson would do . . . if he could."

She surveyed them from her hospital bed for a long time before she responded, urged on by Dupré reminding her that she was in no position to help herself at that precise point in time, and time had a habit of slipping away when men had other problems to face in the near future.

"I don't like to involve you," she said weakly.

They both smiled encouragingly, knowing her resistance to proffered help was about to crumble.

She began to talk.

★ ★ ★

Alfred Layburn greeted them with a smile on his lips, but with eyes that were filled with cautious inquisitiveness.

"Strangers in town?"

"It's been a while," Dupré conceded. "You got a room we can share?"

"Must be your lucky day. Room became vacant an hour ago. Married couple called back east unexpectedly. Wonderful thing, the telegraph, don't you think?"

Dupré nodded in agreement, thinking of the telegraph he had just despatched to Chicago.

Layburn was a big man, with shoulders that reminded Will of a Hereford bull. A mop of wavy, sandy hair topped a rugged face and firm jaw, even though there was the beginning of a double chin beneath the bone. A hard man, Queenie had said, and the cold grey eyes helped to convince Will Foreman that she was not wrong.

Queenie had talked mostly to Henry, with him being the elder and more familiar of her two visitors, and it had been obvious to Will that she would not have been quite so candid if Henry had not been present. The two were more of an age, whereas Will Foreman knew he was at least ten or twelve years younger than Queenie Parsons. He didn't mind, content to sit and listen.

"He's a greedy man, Henry, but he made it clear he wanted me as much as what I'd built up. I expect he's had dozens of women in his time, but he's like a lot of men, what comes easy doesn't excite him that much. He's a bit like you in that respect."

Dupré took no offence and she went on with her story.

"A lot of men have wanted to bed me, as you know full well, but most of them eventually come around to accepting that I'm not a man's woman. I play a man's game as well as most and better than some. Layburn couldn't stomach the idea that I was only interested in being a businesswoman. Told me I just hadn't met the right man to bring the woman out in me, but he didn't like it when I told him *he* wasn't the right man, either."

A big grin stretched Henry Dupré's mouth. He recalled how much he had tried to charm Queenie himself but, as she had said, he had been one of the men who came around to seeing things her way, after which he quit trying.

"Seems like a drastic way to salve injured pride, setting fire to the hotel. You sure you're not letting your dislike of the man colour your judgement, Queenie?"

"Not a bit. That's what he threatened me with if I didn't 'come across', as he called it."

"What *did* he say, exactly?"

"He would talk about the fires we'd had in the town, quite often, and let's face it, Henry, there had been a lot in the early days, before I came here, and he would say it took only one match to destroy everything a man had built up. In my case he meant woman."

Dupré rubbed his chin, still not convinced. "You sure the fire couldn't have been started by accident? A cigar stub not properly deadened late at night?"

"No, Henry. Every night I did a thorough check of the downstairs rooms before I went to bed, and that was *after* I'd locked up and everyone had gone to their rooms."

"Mmm."

"I smelled kerosene when I woke up, but by the time I got dressed the fire already had a good hold and I had to rouse the sleeping guests. Two or three of them were in a drunken sleep and took a lot of rousing."

"Didn't think you tolerated drunks, Queenie."

"I don't. I wasn't meaning objectionably drunk, but men who'd had more than a few and slept heavily as a result."

"You got 'em all out?" Will Foreman interjected.

"Fortunately, but some of them were suffering from smoke inhalation. Some had minor burns, but I seem to have got the worst of it, going back for that cash box."

"But you've still gotten no proof a lawyer could take into court, have you?" Dupré challenged.

"That's a fact, but there's more than one way to skin a skunk."

"True. Very true." Dupré looked at Will. "I guess we'd best go find this skunk, Will."

"I reckon you're right, Mr Dupré."

"He owns 'The Cosmopolitan'," Queenie informed them, "and 'The Miner's Rest', a gambling joint and whorehouse. You'll probably find him at one or the other."

"Right. Anything you need, Queenie?" Dupré asked as he stood up to leave.

"No, but come and see me again before you leave town, will you? I won't ever love you, Henry, but I count you as a friend."

In the hotel room the two men went through what Queenie had told them again, trying to pick holes in the woman's reasoning, wanting to be sure her version of what had occurred was not tainted by emotional stress.

"Even if she was right about it being arson, there's no proof it was Layburn who lit the torch. Queenie could have other enemies, Will."

"Mebbe, but my guess is she's right. Be interestin' to see if he's known in Chicago, but while we wait for a reply to your telegraph, we could nose around some."

"We will do that, in the morning."

"Queenie said Layburn owns the brothel down the street, as well as a few o' the stores in town. Like she said, an ambitious man, greedy for more. Men like that don't usually let scruples stop 'em."

Dupré made no attempt to stifle a yawn.

"I guess you're right, but that's enough conjecture for one day. I'm for some shut-eye. Time to start that probing tomorrow. I'm kinda weary."

Dupré was soon asleep, but Will Foreman's mind was far too active. For Keith Jackson's sake, he had to put right the wrong that had been perpetrated on Queenie Parsons, with a little help from Dupré, only he couldn't yet see how they could set about it.

16

HAVING admitted to themselves at breakfast that gathering any hard evidence against Alfred Layburn seemed fairly remote, they nevertheless resolved to make the effort. Will Foreman agreed to Henry Dupré's suggestion that they should separate and pursue their inquiries individually, meeting up at suppertime to pool their findings. There was not much to share.

"The fire chief told me there was no doubt in his mind that 'Queenie's House' was deliberately set on fire," Dupré began. "The smell of kerosene was strong in the smoke and flames, but the chances of nailing the culprit were about as low as they could get. There were too many folks standing around watching the blaze by the time the fire-fighters got there."

"At least we can be sure Queenie was right when she told us it was calculated arson."

"Yes. I talked to a few people who remembered seeing Layburn amongst the watchers."

"Me too. But nobody who said he tried to join in the rescue bid."

Dupré's mouth was a tight line. "If he was innocent in this affair, I find that strange. When a man takes a fancy to a woman he don't just stand around wondering if she's being burned to death; he rushes in to try and rescue her."

"That what you would've done?"

"I sure would. I like Queenie. Always did."

"Still don't prove he set fire to the place," Will sighed.

"Short of a confession, we won't find hard proof. Looks like we'll have to use a bit of trickery."

"Yeah, but then we figured that right from the start. I guess we'll have to confront him with it. You got a reply from Chicago?"

"I did." Dupré pulled a sheet of paper from his pocket. "Here, read it yourself."

SUBJECT SPENT A YEAR IN JAIL FOR ATTEMPTED MURDER IN NEW YORK 1866 STOP DESERTED WIFE AND TWO DAUGHTERS 1868 STOP SUSPECTED OF ARSON ATTEMPT IN SHELBYVILLE 1873 STOP NEVER CHARGED STOP SUSPECTED SOURCE OF WEALTH ROBBERY BUT NO PROOF STOP

Will handed back the telegraph with the opinion, "Not much to nail him with there."

"No, but it's a start. We can fool him into thinking we know more than we do. Won't be easy to convince him it would be in his interests to compensate Queenie though."

"Watch out, here he comes now," Will warned.

Layburn halted beside their table.

"Good-evening, gentlemen. Supper satisfactory?"

Dupré answered, "Fine, Mr Layburn. You've gotten yourself a good cook back there." He nodded in the direction of the kitchen.

"I choose my staff carefully, Mr Dupré. They're all female, but I don't encourage them to fraternize with the boarders. If you men want a little action, I can recommend 'The Miner's Rest' in the next block. Caters for everything a man might want. Know what I mean?"

"Yeah, we know what you mean," Will acknowledged. "We'd thought o' lookin' in later. I believe you own the place?"

Layburn's smile was broad. "That I do, Mr Foreman, that I do. I also own three stores in town. I'm a very respected citizen in Ellsworth. I'll look out for you later. I'm just off to the 'Miner's'."

"We'll look you up, Mr Layburn."

"Call me Alf. Everybody does."

He turned and left them, heading for the street.

"I vote we waste no more time," Will suggested. "Let's nail him tonight."

"I'll second that vote, Mr Foreman. You prepared in case it gets rough?"

"Don't fancy a fist fight with that great hulk, if that's what you, mean, not in my present condition. I'll let my forty-four do the talkin', if it should come to that."

"Let's give it an hour. I like my supper to digest nice and quietly before I get involved in rough stuff."

He pulled a cheroot from his pocket, poked it between his teeth, and struck a lucifer.

★ ★ ★

The place was a hive of activity. Layburn had spent a lot of money fitting out the place. Mahogany bar, with wide mirrors reflecting a large array of liquor bottles; roulette wheel, blackjack table, poker games, faro, and good-looking young women in a variety of colourful, revealing dresses to excite the customers. A stairway led to upstairs rooms, where men were treated to all the sexual bliss they could fantasize about, willing to overlook the dent in their wallets.

Dupré and Foreman ambled to the bar and were soon accosted individually.

"Not right now, girlie," Dupré said politely. "We only came in on business. We've an appointment with your boss."

"Oh!" the redhead returned with a smile. "Maybe later?"

"Maybe."

Will was not quite so abrupt. Keith Jackson had taught him to use saloon women as sources of information, and he bought the brunette by his side a drink. Dupré did not interfere and moved off towards the roulette wheel to watch the play.

"You gotta name, handsome?"

"Will Foreman. You?"

"Vicci."

"Short for Victoria?"

"Yes. Victoria Maria Oliver, if you want to be precise."

Will smiled with false pleasure. "I like that."

"You're new in town."

"Got in yesterday. You worked here long, Vicci?"

"Almost two years. And believe me, that's good for this place. Most girls quit in the first year."

"Really? You surprise me."

"That's because you don't know Alf Layburn. I don't know what your business is with him, but I'll lay odds he'll screw you."

Will laughed. "I'd hate to take your money. Me an' my friend Henry don't get screwed."

"Like I said, you don't know Alf."

"Tell me about Alf. I gather you don't like him much."

"No. He used me the way he uses all the girls who come to work here."

"How exactly?"

"He starts off by making a girl feel special. Treats her like a queen. Makes her his personal mistress; tells her to be pleasant to the customers but not to take any of them upstairs. 'That's for the others, honey, not you,' he says. Then he fancies someone new, so we all end up the same."

"That's why they leave?"

"Mostly, only a girl can still put a bit by, even after Alf has taken his cut, so they hang on until they've gotten what they need to move on."

"Does that mean you haven't made your pile yet?"

"I guess it means I want a bigger pile than most, but I'm one of the few who can swallow her pride, forget hurt feelings, and make what I can. I do my job well, and Alf knows it. Hey! Why am I telling you all this?"

Will flashed his teeth again. "You must be the friendly type."

"Hmm! Must be those big brown eyes of yours. You know you're the best-looking man I've seen in here in a month!"

He put on a heavy sigh to indicate regret. "I guess it's as well I'm only here for a day or two. Talk like that can get a girl most any place with me."

"Well forget what I just told you, will you? Please?"

"My lips are sealed."

"You sure you don't want to go upstairs a while?"

"I'd love to," he lied shamelessly, "but I see your boss is already talkin' with Henry. I'd best join them."

"Shame. I wouldn't have charged you, Will. I fancy you something rotten."

"I'll remember that. Never knew I had such charm."

He drained his glass, gave her an encouraging smile, then moved to join Dupré. Just as he did so a fight broke out in the far corner of the bar room and Layburn left Dupré to go and sort it out. The two men watched as

Layburn used his immense strength to part the men and order them outside. Reluctantly they went, their glares of anger now directed at the big man instead of each other. Will guessed they had seen Layburn in action at some other time and did not relish being hit by those ham-like hands.

"I see what you mean about not wanting to get into a fist fight with him," Dupré told Will. "He scared them two without even trying."

"Don't reckon he worries too much about Queensberry rules, either. I reckon he could fell a steer with one punch."

"A slight exaggeration, Will, but I get your drift."

They watched with interest as Layburn moved around, accepting the complimentary words tossed his way with a beaming smile, much of them of the fawning variety. Eventually he returned to Will and Henry.

"I've built a reputation here for

keeping a quiet house," he told them. "Stop trouble before it gets out of hand and it saves having the place wrecked by men just looking for an excuse for a brawl." He smirked with pride. "Don't ever need to call in the law to arrest anybody."

"A wise policy," Dupré commented. "Er . . . could we talk in private some place?"

A puzzled frown creased Layburn's brow, but an instinct for knowledge prompted him to accede to the request. "I have an office upstairs. Come on up."

They followed him, with Will Foreman feeling a tensing of stomach muscles. He looked at Dupré, but the little man seemed perfectly at his ease. Will decided to let him take the lead in the discussion.

"Take a seat, gentlemen," Layburn invited, settling himself behind an ornate desk. "What can I do for you?"

"We'd like to talk about fire,"

Dupré opened, easing himself into a comfortable chair.

"Fire!"

"Fire. A couple of cans of kerosene and a match could make a right mess of this place, Mr Layburn, and in your boots I wouldn't fancy the prospect."

The cold grey eyes hardened. "Is this a shakedown?"

"You might call it that. I'd prefer to think of it as a friendly discussion. No sense in either of us getting sore. Wouldn't do any good."

"Friendly discussion! Don't sound much like it to me. You come in here . . . "

Dupré cut in, "There was a fire down the street about three weeks ago, if you recall, Mr Layburn? 'Queenie's House'. You stood and watched it gutted."

"How do you know that?"

Dupré looked across at Will, seated at a well-chosen angle, before answering. "We know a lot about you, Mr

Layburn. We know where you came from, what you did before you came to Ellsworth, about your wife and two small daughters, the time you spent in jail . . . Want me to go on?"

Layburn's face began to look flushed. "Who the hell are you?"

"We told you last night when we came to the hotel. I'm Henry Dupré and my buddy here is Will Foreman."

"That's not what I meant and you know it!" Layburn snarled.

Ignoring the protest, Will said, "There's something Henry didn't mention . . . the sister of a friend of ours. She killed herself after you turned her into a prostitute. We don't like that too much."

It was a massive gamble on Will's part, but it seemed to strike a chord in Layburn.

"Who?" The saloon owner's hesitancy indicated a disquiet in his mind. "Who is this girl?"

"Aw, come on, you cain't pretend

you don't know who she was!"

Layburn tried to dismiss the accusation with a shrug. "I can't be held responsible for every girl who comes to work here. I pay them well. They don't have to open their legs if they don't want to. I don't put a gun to their heads."

"But you do bed them yourself before you set them to work, don't you? Then tell them all men are the same in the dark? Coax them with the prospects of extra money?"

Another shrug of the shoulders and an attempt at a knowing smile. "You're both men who've been around. The girls I engage are all good-lookers, and I'm only human, same as you. What do you think I am, a monk or something?"

Will shook his head. "That you are not. You're a fornicating, thieving, malicious skunk, an' you're about to pay for your latest misdeed."

Layburn jumped to his feet and snarled, "Now listen to me, you young puppy, I don't take that kind o'talk from anybody!"

He pointed to the door with the index finger of his right hand extended. "Now you get the hell out of here before I throw you out!"

Will Foreman filled his right hand with his Colt .44 pistol, tipped back his hat, and nonchalantly eased himself in his chair. "Let's not get excited, Mr Layburn. Like Henry said, we jest want a friendly discussion."

Suddenly lost for words, his eyes flickering from Will's gaze to the gun pointing in his direction, Layburn slumped back into his chair.

"All right, let's get it over with. What do you want?"

Dupré answered. "Compensation for Queenie Parsons. We know you threatened her; we know it was criminal arson; we know you stood and watched her place burn while she was inside it; we know you never lifted a finger to help her. *You* put a torch to her place and *you* are going to come up with the money to cover her loss. Around twenty grand would be about right, I reckon."

"*Twenty thousand dollars!* You must be crazy!"

"Not that much to a man who owns three stores, a hotel *and* this place. Like I indicated earlier, a few matches and some kerosene can do a lot of damage."

"You wouldn't dare!"

"Think not? Are you that much of a gambling man?"

The expensively furnished office took on an atmosphere of tense expectancy, mounting to a crescendo of unbearable severity, with none of the three men knowing just what would break it. Will Foreman took comfort from the gun in his hand, slanting a quick glance at Dupré and admiring the little man's seemingly nerveless acceptance of the situation. It was Henry who broke the spell.

"Twenty thousand dollars, in cash, will do very nicely, Mr Layburn."

Will wondered if the man had a hidden Derringer in an inside pocket, but he gave no indication of it. He seemed afraid of the gun pointing towards him and Dupré's show of supreme confidence. Will could see right through him as Layburn searched his mind for a way of escape, fuelled by a fury he could hardly control.

"I don't keep that kind of cash on hand. You must know that."

"We'll take what you've gotten in that safe for now," Dupré told him. "You can go to the bank in the morning for the rest."

His only chance was to humour these men, Layburn decided. Try to gain some time. "I'll give you a banker's draft, made out to Queenie."

"Uhuh. Cash money. Get the safe open, count out the money, put it in an envelope addressed to Mrs Parsons, then you can't accuse us of coming in here and robbing you at gun-point. Like I said, you can get the balance in the morning."

Layburn sat staring from one to the other, still wracking his brains to find a way out of his predicament. The unblinking stares of the two men, who seemed unmoved by his hesitancy, sapped his resolve. Will offered him a little more persuasion.

"You wouldn't want the folks in Ellsworth to know about your wife an' two daughters, livin' in poverty, would you now, Mr Layburn? You wouldn't remain a very respected citizen for long once that got around. They might run you out o' town, then you'd have nothing."

"Or about the girl you drove to suicide," Dupré added, piling on the pressure.

"All right," Layburn conceded, "on one condition. After you get . . . "

"You ain't in no position to lay down conditions," Will told him.

"But . . . "

Dupré said, "You want to know if we'll leave town once you've paid your debt to Queenie, is that it?"

"Yes, that's it."

"You have my word on it."

Layburn looked across at Will for confirmation.

"And mine, only I'd like it better if you sent some money to your family every once in a while. It'd sorta ease my conscience."

"*Your* conscience!"

"Yeah. I'm kinda funny that way."

There was a long silence as Layburn stared hard at Will, unable to fathom what was going on in the mind of the younger man. At the same time he feared the revelations the two men might make to the citizens of Ellsworth. Slowly he turned his back on them and unlocked the safe.

He counted out six thousand dollars, addressed an envelope to Queenie Parsons, and put the money inside, sealing it before tossing it to Henry Dupré.

"Satisfied?" he asked with a bad-tempered snarl.

"You've been very co-operative, Mr

Layburn. I was afraid Will might have to put a bullet in your guts before you were willing to see sense."

Dupré stowed the envelope in an inside coat pocket. "We'll leave you now, only we'd be obliged if you sat there long enough for us to get back to the hotel and up to our rooms. You savvy?"

"You make yourself abundantly clear, Mr Dupré."

"Good."

Will holstered his gun as he eased himself up from the chair, but he took the precaution of walking backwards to the door, just in case Layburn had a shooter hidden close to hand. Before leaving he said, "We'll make arrangements about collectin' the balance in the mornin'. Don't even think o' renegin' on the deal. I wouldn't like that. See you at breakfast. Best have our bill ready. We won't be stayin' around long."

Back in the hotel room Dupré turned to Will and queried, "When did you find out about that girl killing herself?"

"I didn't. It was jest a wild guess that one o' them had been driven to it at some time."

"There's more to you than I figured, Will Foreman."

Will grinned back at him. "Yes, Henry, there is."

17

THEY talked for half an hour, knowing that Alfred Layburn would not just sit back and accept the loss of twenty thousand dollars without a fight. At that moment they had the upper hand, but when and how would Layburn try to wrest it from them?

"He'll know men in Ellsworth ready and willing to do a sneaky cutting-down job, but time is not on his side," Dupré mused. "He's got to get rid of both of us before we get to the bank in the morning."

"I figure he'll leave us alone tonight to try an' lead us into a false sense o' security; let us believe we've gotten him over a barrel an' that he accepts that he's gotta pay. He'll have some gunny try t'pick us off in the mornin'."

"We can't be sure of that, Will. He

might have somebody burst in on us between three and four in the morning. It's well known that for a lot of folks, that's the hour when they're in their deepest sleep, and he'll have a master key to every door. Killing sleeping men is easy. We'd best move both beds, so we won't be where we're expected to be, and then take shifts for sleeping."

Will accepted the logic of Dupré's reasoning and the two of them lifted their beds and placed them head first against the opposite wall, one either side of the door. They tossed a coin to see who would take the first watch, resulting in Will settling down to sleep first, his gun handy in readiness for a sudden awakening.

They agreed to remain fully dressed and to hell with a crumpled shirt.

"Best keep your boots on, too," Dupré advised.

They would only be trying to sleep for four hours in turn. Dupré took the key out of the lock to make it easy for Layburn or his hired assassin to insert another key from outside, then settled down to wait, his back propped against the bed-head, gun by his side, just inches away from his hand. He was half hoping Layburn would make his play during the night, reasoning that having lost the battle of wills in the evening, losing a noisy action with guns would convince him he was up against men who were determined not to be defeated. If nothing happened before breakfast, then the dangers of being shot down in the street in broad daylight would mount considerably. Dupré was convinced that not only did Alfred Layburn have no intention of handing over another fourteen thousand dollars, but he would also plan to recover the six thousand already surrendered.

* * *

They came during the hour Dupré had predicted. The sound of the door knob being gently turned was enough to alert

Will Foreman, now having replaced Dupré as watchdog. In the darkness Will palmed his .44 as he heard the careful insertion of a key in the lock. He slid off the bed and shook Dupré. The little man was instantly alert and Will catfooted back to his own side of the door just as it was flung open and two guns belched flame and lead in the direction of where the beds should have been.

Neither Dupré nor Will made a move until the attackers had emptied their guns, then turned and fled along the landing for a planned getaway. As they reached the head of the stairway they were cut short in their stride as bullets hit them from behind. One man jerked violently, like a puppet on a string, then fell to the landing floor. The other gunman tumbled noisily down the stairs.

An eerie silence settled on the hotel moments after the cacophony of gunfire ended, then men rushed out from bedroom doors to investigate the reason for having their sleep disturbed. Most of them were still in their underwear or wearing nightshirts, but some had guns in their hands to protect themselves should the need arise.

Will Foreman stood over the man on the landing, while Dupré dashed down the stairs to make sure there was no further danger from the other gunman. He came face to face with Alfred Layburn, fully dressed, a gun in his hand.

"Nice try, Layburn, but we ain't as dumb as you thought." He glanced down at the form huddled at his feet. "Your hired gun looks dead to me. Maybe you'd best make sure."

Fury blazed in Layburn's eyes, his mouth distorted in a snarl of hate, but men were coming down the stairs and his impulse to shoot Dupré on the spot quickly died as he lowered his gun.

"What the hell's goin' on?" the first man down demanded. "What kind of a hotel are you running here, Layburn?"

"I'm sorry, Mr Pulford, but I'm as

mystified as you are. Maybe Mr Dupré can shed some light on the matter? It was you who shot this man, wasn't it, Mr Dupré?"

"It was, but what I want to know is how he managed to get hold of a key to my room, Mr Layburn. He's an assassin. Him and his partner up on the landing filled our room with bullets in an attempt to kill me and Mr Foreman."

"That what happened?" Pulford seemed ready to accept Dupré's explanation, even though his questioning gaze indicated his curiosity. Then he looked at Layburn. "I guess you forgot to lock up properly, Mr Layburn."

Unsure of himself, Layburn floundered. "Looks that way, but I could've sworn . . . "

"I guess we all make mistakes," Dupré said as Layburn hesitated.

Their eyes held in a long stare, the message in Dupré's easily understood by the hotel man.

"Don't think I've ever made a

mistake like that before," Layburn said, switching his eyes to Pulford. "Would you check the front door for me, Mr Pulford? I'll take a look in back."

Will Foreman had now joined his pard at the foot of the stairs. "The one upstairs is dead, Henry."

"And this one. If the bullets didn't kill him I guess the fall did. His neck looks like it could be broken."

"Say! Don't you fellers take your clothes off when you go to bed?" one of the other guests remarked.

"We'd been playing cards," Dupré said with a disarming smile. "Will, would you take a look and see what damage these gunmen caused?"

Will understood the message and ran back up the stairway. Their room door was wide open. He went in and closed it, pulled a match from his pocket and lit the lamp. Bullet holes had pockmarked the far wall, just where the beds had previously been placed.

Downstairs the questions were flying

at Dupré thick and fast.

"Who are these men?"

"What did they want?"

"Why would they be shootin' at you?"

"We'd better get the sheriff!"

"Ain't a man safe in his bed in this hotel?"

"I'm gettin' outa here!"

Glenn Pulford came back and reported that the front door of the hotel was securely locked, then Layburn returned, looking apologetic.

"I'm very sorry you've all been disturbed, gentlemen. They got in through the kitchen. You men with wives with you had best get back to your rooms to reassure them that everything is now under control. Mr Dupré, would you go and get the sheriff for me? I'll have to report this incident; find out who these men are and what they were doing here."

"We know what they were doing here," one man said. "They came to kill Dupré!"

208

Layburn said, "Is that a fact?" His eyes slid back to Dupré. "I wonder why?"

"Yeah, so do I! Who are you, Dupré?"

Dupré offered them all a relaxed smile. "I'm an undercover agent, but with these two men dead, I guess there's no longer any need for secrecy. Maybe *you* should go for the sheriff! Mr Layburn, seeing as you're dressed and this is your hotel."

For a moment it looked as if Layburn was looking for some excuse not to go out, but then he saw the others giving him odd looks and decided he was best out of the way until they had returned to their beds.

"I won't be long, Mr Dupré. Will you keep an eye on things until I get back?"

"My pleasure."

"The rest of you gentlemen should go and get some sleep. I'll have everything back to normal in time for breakfast."

He turned away and went out the

back in sudden haste, leaving Dupré to ponder on what tale he could cook up for the sheriff before he got back. The lawman was probably asleep anyway and would not be pleased by being disturbed.

Will Foreman came back down the stairs as the other men went up to their rooms.

* * *

"You know these men, Dupré?" the sheriff asked sharply.

"No, Sheriff they're both strangers to me."

"How about you, Foreman?"

"They look familiar, but I cain't say as I know them, either one."

"Why would they come in here and try to kill you while you slept?"

"I guess it could've been one of two reasons," Will answered calmly. "I'm carryin' a lot o' money; Henry here is a Pinkerton man. Could be somebody wanted Henry out o' the way, or mebbe it was a plain attempt at robbery. My guess is they were after Henry, otherwise why did they run? Whatever, their plan to kill us came unstuck."

He threw a hard look at Alfred Layburn, the warning in his brown eyes plain enough to be understood.

The sheriff turned to Layburn. "That satisfy you?"

"What do you know about these men, Sheriff?"

"A couple of no-accounts, from what I've seen of them. They come and go, and although there's nothing known against them, I've had them figured as a couple of hustlers. You got a room we can put both bodies in 'til morning, Mr Layburn? I'll get the mortician to collect them as soon as he can."

"I suppose so. I'll show you. There's a store room in back. Not much room in there, but if it's only for a few hours . . . "

Will and Dupré carried the dead gunmen into the store room and laid them side by side, having to climb over them to get out again. Blood smeared the floor.

"There's blood on the landin' an' at the foot o' the stairs," Will told Layburn, "only don't ask me t'clean it up, will ya? I ain't best pleased with your security in this hotel. If'n I'd been asleep when they busted in it might've been me lyin' dead in there now."

"I have already apologized, Foreman. What more can I do?"

"You can get my bill ready. I'll be leavin' right after breakfast."

"I'll talk with you later, Layburn," Dupré advised him. "About that business we discussed last evening?"

The sheriff missed the blistering hate in Layburn's silent response as he turned for the door.

"Good night, gentlemen. I'm heading back to my bed."

18

"YOU think it's safe to eat this grub?" Will queried, looking earnestly at Dupré.

"I think so. Hardly likely Layburn would risk poisoning the wrong resident, even if he had any obnoxious substance to hand. The waitress or the cook would have to be in on any idea of that nature, and that redhead who brought our plates seemed normal enough to me."

Will forked a portion and sniffed. "Smells all right." Gingerly he pushed the food into his mouth. "Tastes normal."

"The condemned man ate a hearty breakfast," Dupré said with a wide smile.

"Cain't say as I allus appreciate your sense o' humour, Henry."

In a more serious vein Dupré

213

responded, "I don't think Layburn will make another attempt to get rid of us. That sheriff would get mighty suspicious if he did, and our brothel-keeper ain't as well respected in this town as he likes to think. If anything happens to us after that early morning attack, a lot of questions would be asked."

"He ain't gonna give in without makin' some attempt to get his money back."

Dupré pushed a reassuring grin across the table. "Enjoy your breakfast. We have to hand it to Layburn, he does know his business."

They began to eat with more confidence.

Layburn approached as they cleared their plates and reached for the coffee. He took a vacant chair and sat down, his face a mask.

"Looks like you picked the wrong men to get your money back last night," Dupré began. "They lost their nerve after they'd emptied their guns,

214

or did you keep them in the dark about that six thousand? Planned to collect it yourself after you'd made sure we were dead, had you?"

Layburn's eyes were smouldering but he found no words to reply.

"Now then," Dupré went on, "about the rest of that money you owe Queenie . . . "

"I owe Queenie Parsons nothing! It's a pity she didn't fry in that place of hers!" The words were spoken softly, little more than a whisper, but the venom in them was manifestly plain.

"That kind o'talk ain't gonna get you no place," Will told him with equal forthrightness.

The calm voice of Henry Dupré went on as if there had never been any interruption. "I shall accompany you to the bank and you will introduce me to the president as Queenie's agent, there to see the transaction through. To save drawing all that cash from the teller, we'll arrange for fourteen thousand dollars to be transferred from your account to Queenie's, with my signature on the papers on her behalf, just so that everything will be nice and legal."

"And how do I explain this transfer to the president?" Layburn asked with a sneer.

"You will tell him it is money loaned to you by Queenie to get you started when you first moved into Ellsworth."

"You think the man is a fool? He knows Queenie never had that kind o' money to lend me!"

"I'll admit that might prompt a few questions, but you don't have to go into details. Give the impression that the original loan was followed by investments in your own projects, in case anything went wrong with her own plans. Now that Queenie is homeless, recovering from burns and in need of the money, you feel it is the right time to let her cash in on her investments. One good turn deserves another, sort of thing. Any more questions?"

"One day I'll get you for this,

Dupré!" His eyes swivelled. "And you, Foreman!"

"Thanks for the warning. I'll have my lawyer put it in my last will and testament."

"Meet me at your front door at eleven," Dupré told Layburn. "Have the bodies gone yet?"

"Yes. Why eleven? Why not now?"

"I have things to do first." Dupré stood up. "See you then. Come on, Will."

Together the two men went to the front door of the hotel and out into the street, ready to put the next stage of their plan into operation.

A block away from the hotel they separated. Will went on alone towards the bank, while Dupré watched his back, even though he was confident no one would try to stop Will. If he was wrong it would not be the first time, and it was just possible that Layburn had been out early to grease the palm of some other gunny whose love of money outweighed his scruples.

Nothing happened.

Will returned fifteen minutes later. "All done. The money is now in Queenie's account."

"Good. Now back to the hotel, pay our bills, then you get down to the livery and take our horses to the railhead. Soon as you see me coming, get them into the box-car. I should have time to make it before the train pulls out for Denver."

★ ★ ★

As both men had suspected he would, the bank president displayed a blatant curiosity at what seemed, on the surface, a very generous gesture on Alfred Layburn's part. Queenie Parsons' rejected suitor put on a smile to try to fool the man behind the desk, but Henry Dupré knew the bank man was not fooled. His comment confirmed it.

"I'm surprised Mrs Parsons kept so much loose cash around. I must warn her against such practices. There are too many desperadoes around who might discover her carelessness."

"You misunderstand, sir," Dupré said, with a sideways glance at Layburn. "Mr Layburn allowed Mrs Parsons to buy an interest in his own business ventures and, as you are well aware, he has been very successful."

As previously instructed by Dupré, Layburn said, "She did not give me this money in a lump sum. A little at a time, as she could afford it, so I would not advise you to make such a suggestion. The lady is entitled to do as she wishes with her own money."

The transaction went through smoothly.

"This must be Mrs Parsons' lucky day. We had a man in earlier donating six thousand to help her get started again, once she is fit and out of hospital. A very popular lady, it seems."

"That's what comes of being honest and fair with folks," Dupré said by way of justification. "Friends rally round when someone like that falls on hard times."

"Just so, Mr Dupré, just so. Have you known her long?"

"Several years, as a matter of fact. You could say we're old friends. That was a terrible thing to happen to such a nice lady."

"It was indeed. Oh, by the way, Mr Layburn, the young man who deposited the six thousand wanted to remain anonymous. You wouldn't know him, by any chance?"

"No, I wouldn't."

"A tall, handsome man with brown hair?"

"Ah! A man fitting that description stayed at the hotel last night. He did mention he was carrying a large sum of money. Wanted to be sure he would not be disturbed during his stay." Layburn put on an exaggerated sigh. "Unfortunately he was, I'm sorry to say. Still, he managed to get the money to you."

"Must be the same man."

"Yes, I would think so. You can tell Queenie about the transfer from my account. We're sadly not on speaking terms at the moment, but she'll understand perfectly."

"I'm sure. Pity about the rift, though. I'll be paying her a visit this evening, as I promised the young man. It will be a blessing to be able to give her so much good news. Might cheer her up."

"That it will," Dupré offered as his parting shot. "Would you make my apologies for me? I promised to go and see her again, but unfortunately I have to leave town right away."

There was a smile on his lips and a singing in his heart at the thought of a wrong rectified. Two men had died violently in the process, but Dupré didn't give a damn.

Out on the street once more he said, "Go back to your hotel, Layburn. I don't fancy you following me."

"I'll never forget you, Dupré. My day will come," Layburn threatened.

"I do love an optimist, but then I

happen to be one. S'long, Layburn."

He watched as the big man walked away, then Dupré headed for the railhead at a run.

★ ★ ★

"Pity we couldn't have told Queenie ourselves," Will said with a regretful sigh as the train pulled out of Ellsworth.

"She'll have a smile as wide as the Grand Canyon when that feller from the bank tells her the good news, though I think Queenie would be well advised to leave Ellsworth after this."

"You think Layburn will have another go at her?"

"I'd bet on it. Think I'll get a letter off to her before I leave Denver."

"I guess she'll be glad of an explanation, though I reckon she'll guess we put the frighteners on Layburn when the bank president tells her where all that money came from."

"Sure she will. Queenie is no fool."

The train gathered speed as the two

men gazed out of the window.

"You got plans, Henry?"

"Expect there'll be a message from Chicago any day now. How about you?"

"I'll go back an' see Mr Jackson, then I guess I owe it to David Clay to get back to that job he kept open for me."

"Think you'll be up to it?"

"Only one way to find out." He threw a knowing grin at Dupré. "Did I tell you he has a real nice-lookin' daughter, Henry?"

"Yes, Will, you did." He yawned. "Think I'll catch up on some lost sleep."

He closed his eyes and let the events of the last few days slip away from him, but Will was not a bit sleepy. Later it would catch up with him, but first he had to decide whether or not he would tell Keith Jackson about what had happened to his old friend, Queenie Parsons.

He came to the conclusion the old

man had enough troubles without being given the news that Queenie would, henceforth, be wearing a wig in place of all that beautiful hair that had been her crowning glory.

His thoughts switched from the old man to the young Henrietta Clay. A serenity spread through him, but he was unaware of the smile that formed on his lips as the train rumbled on.

THE END

FIGHTING RAMROD
Charles N. Heckelmann

Most men would have cut their losses, but Frazer counted the bullets in his guns and said he'd soak the range in blood before he'd give up another inch of what was his.

LONE GUN
Eric Allen

Smoke Blackbird had been away too long. The Lequires had seized the Blackbird farm, forcing the Indians and settlers off, and no one seemed willing to fight! He had to fight alone.

THE THIRD RIDER
Barry Cord

Mel Rawlins wasn't going to let anything stand in his way. His father was murdered, his two brothers gone. Now Mel rode for vengeance.

ARIZONA DRIFTERS
W. C. Tuttle

When drifting Dutton and Lonnie Steelman decide to become partners they find that they have a common enemy in the formidable Thurston brothers.

TOMBSTONE
Matt Braun

Wells Fargo paid Luke Starbuck to outgun the silver-thieving stagecoach gang at Tombstone. Before long Luke can see the only thing bearing fruit in this eldorado will be the gallows tree.

HIGH BORDER RIDERS
Lee Floren

Buckshot McKee and Tortilla Joe cut the trail of a border tough who was running Mexican beef into Texas. They stopped the smuggler in his tracks.

BRETT RANDALL, GAMBLER
E. B. Mann

Larry Day had the choice of running away from the law or of assuming a dead man's place. No matter what he decided he was bound to end up dead.

THE GUNSHARP
William R. Cox

The Eggerleys weren't very smart. They trained their sights on Will Carney and Arizona's biggest blood bath began.

THE DEPUTY OF SAN RIANO
Lawrence A. Keating and
Al. P. Nelson

When a man fell dead from his horse, Ed Grant was spotted riding away from the scene. The deputy sheriff rode out after him and came up against everything from gunfire to dynamite.

FARGO: MASSACRE RIVER
John Benteen

The ambushers up ahead had now blocked the road. Fargo's convoy was a jumble, a perfect target for the insurgents' weapons!

SUNDANCE: DEATH IN THE LAVA
John Benteen

The Modoc's captured the wagon train and its cargo of gold. But now the halfbreed they called Sundance was going after it . . .

HARSH RECKONING
Phil Ketchum

Five years of keeping himself alive in a brutal prison had made Brand tough and careless about who he gunned down . . .

FARGO: PANAMA GOLD
John Benteen

With foreign money behind him, Buckner was going to destroy the Panama Canal before it could be completed. Fargo's job was to stop Buckner.

FARGO:
THE SHARPSHOOTERS
John Benteen

The Canfield clan, thirty strong were raising hell in Texas. Fargo was tough enough to hold his own against the whole clan.

PISTOL LAW
Paul Evan Lehman

Lance Jones came back to Mustang for just one thing — revenge! Revenge on the people who had him thrown in jail.

HELL RIDERS
Steve Mensing

Wade Walker's kid brother, Duane, was locked up in the Silver City jail facing a rope at dawn. Wade was a ruthless outlaw, but he was smart, and he had vowed to have his brother out of jail before morning!

DESERT OF THE DAMNED
Nelson Nye

The law was after him for the murder of a marshal — a murder he didn't commit. Breen was after him for revenge — and Breen wouldn't stop at anything . . . blackmail, a frameup . . . or murder.

DAY OF THE COMANCHEROS
Steven C. Lawrence

Their very name struck terror into men's hearts — the Comancheros, a savage army of cutthroats who swept across Texas, leaving behind a bloodstained trail of robbery and murder.

SUNDANCE: SILENT ENEMY
John Benteen

was on a
needed to
ne crazed
undance.

Jack Slade

Lassiter wasn't the kind of man to listen to reason. Cross him once and he'll hold a grudge for years to come — if he let you live that long.

LAST STAGE TO GOMORRAH
Barry Cord

Jeff Carter, tough ex-riverboat gambler, now had himself a horse ranch that kept him free from gunfights and card games. Until Sturvesant of Wells Fargo showed up.